Echoes of war drifted uphill

"Time for the second act," Mack Bolan said, displaying the long blade he'd taken from Felix Giamante's boot sheath.

"They'll see us!" the hardman hissed.

"That's the idea."

The sound of angry voices reached them, calling back and forth like hunters flushing out game. In a moment the Sinistra gunners would tumble into the clearing and find the car.

"You've got to give me a weapon," Giamante demanded.

"Sure." Bolan offered him an old Browning that he'd picked up from one of the slain Sinistra clansmen. "But in case you're thinking about killing *me,* you're a few rounds light." The Executioner held up the clip of bullets for the emptied pistol.

Automatic bursts streaked through the darkness, scything the trees and brush, tearing loose bark and small branches, drilling through the fenders of Giamante's spotless sports car.

"Live through this and you might be worth talking to," Bolan said. He tossed his enemy the clip and vanished into the trees.

The war he started between Sinistra and the Giamante Family raged on behind him.

MACK BOLAN®

The Executioner

DON PENDLETON'S

THE EXECUTIONER®

FEATURING MACK BOLAN®

RANSOM RUN

A GOLD EAGLE BOOK FROM

WORLDWIDE®

TORONTO • NEW YORK • LONDON
AMSTERDAM • PARIS • SYDNEY • HAMBURG
STOCKHOLM • ATHENS • TOKYO • MILAN
MADRID • WARSAW • BUDAPEST • AUCKLAND

First edition August 1993

ISBN 0-373-61176-5

Special thanks and acknowledgment to
Rich Rainey for his contribution to this work.

RANSOM RUN

Those who will not reason
Perish in the act.
Those who will not act
Perish for that reason.
—W. H. Auden

My reason tells me that the savages need another
lesson to keep them in their place. The time has come
to act and act decisively. Whatever lies ahead, I trust
my instinct and my stars. Let those who feed on
human misery perish in the cleansing fire.
—Mack Bolan

THE
MACK BOLAN®
LEGEND

Nothing less than a war could have fashioned the destiny of the man called Mack Bolan. Bolan earned the Executioner title in the jungle hell of Vietnam.

But this soldier also wore another name—Sergeant Mercy. He was so tagged because of the compassion he showed to wounded comrades-in-arms and Vietnamese civilians.

Mack Bolan's second tour of duty ended prematurely when he was given emergency leave to return home and bury his family, victims of the Mob. Then he declared a one-man war against the Mafia.

He confronted the Families head-on from coast to coast, and soon a hope of victory began to appear. But Bolan had broken society's every rule. That same society started gunning for this elusive warrior—to no avail.

So Bolan was offered amnesty to work within the system against terrorism. This time, as an employee of Uncle Sam, Bolan became Colonel John Phoenix. With a command center at Stony Man Farm in Virginia, he and his new allies—Able Team and Phoenix Force—waged relentless war on a new adversary: the KGB.

But when his one true love, April Rose, died at the hands of the Soviet terror machine, Bolan severed all ties with Establishment authority.

Now, after a lengthy lone-wolf struggle and much soul-searching, the Executioner has agreed to enter an "arm's-length" alliance with his government once more, reserving the right to pursue personal missions in his Everlasting War.

PROLOGUE

Lake Como, Italy

The reinforced tires of the armored Mercedes crushed the pastel-colored stones of the circular driveway deeper into the gravel bed.

Except for the driveway, the lakeside retreat looked like an ancient Roman villa snatched from the past and dropped intact onto one of the most expensive parcels of earth in the north of Italy.

Tall fluted columns braced an ornate balustrade that led to the main entrance, a platform wide enough for Caesar himself to address the multitudes.

Standing guard at the gate was Alfredo Galantine, an armed bodyguard in a sleek-fitting suit, who watched the Mercedes through the sidelight windows at the front door of the villa. Galantine relaxed when he saw the driver step out of the car with a large soft leather portfolio, the kind favored by architects, advertising men and fashion designers, all of whom had carried their precious scrolls into Villa Condorri at one time or another.

The man with the portfolio was outfitted with a suit that could have come direct from the Condorri flagship boutique on Via della Spiga, the center of Milan's fashion district. He moved with the step of a man accustomed to giving orders, and he had the feral look of a man not to be trifled with on his way up the corporate ladder, a man eager to take heads at every chance.

His associate was also well dressed, if a bit rougher on the edges. Despite the suit, the other man looked like he was muscle for the Mercedes's owner. The hardman smiled. The bodyguard was light-years removed from Galantine's caste, not as refined nor as sleek, a bull in search of a red flag.

Galantine smiled, deciding that he would have to show them what a professional security man was like.

He opened the door before either of the men could reach the steps, taking them slightly by surprise. Both men stopped and studied Galantine from the tip of his well-manicured crown to the hand that rested close to the holster on his hip, like a soldier with a spear barring their path.

"Yes?" Galantine inquired in a voice that added a chill to the hot summer air.

"I have something for Mr. Condorri," the man said, raising the portfolio in front of him.

"He is busy. And I've heard nothing about this."

The man smiled. "Imagine that. We've just completed the drawings for an entire new line of clothing. A most secretive project that, perhaps, just perhaps, Mr. Condorri didn't feel the need to let his doorman in on."

Galantine's face reddened. He'd learned years ago that the rich were different. A fair share of them were total bastards. He'd also learned not to be intimidated by them. He dismissed the muscle with a glance, then settled his gaze on the man with the portfolio. "And you are?"

"Amory Faust."

"And what do you have for Mr. Condorri?"

"Here," Faust said, reaching into the portfolio, "you can give him a sample."

Galantine nodded.

Then he stepped back, but it was too late.

Black steel flashed in the sunlight as Faust removed a compact Ingram machine pistol with a sound suppressor threaded onto the end of it, pulling the trigger just as the blunt snout cleared the leather case.

The first 9 mm slug chipped off a piece of the door. The second blew a piece off the right side of Galantine's skull, pinwheeling it into the air like a bloodied stone. The third slug cored his temple, and the hardman staggered back into the house, dropping dead onto the priceless antique carpet.

Three rounds and he was out.

A backup car pulled up behind the Mercedes, doors flapping open like wings. Four men spilled from the vehicle and trotted toward the villa, splitting up two on each side, winding their way through the heavily forested and landscaped grounds. All carried automatic weapons, like heavy metal gardeners ready to scythe down anything that stood in their way.

Amory Faust, or the man his Sinistra paymasters knew as Amory Faust, stepped inside the villa. The barrel of the machine pistol nosed ahead of him as he moved from room to room. When he climbed the winding staircase, the silenced barrel of the lightweight Ingram pointed straight up like a periscope.

But there the waters were untroubled.

Neither Faust nor Donato, the top man from the squad he'd brought with him, encountered a soul in the villa. Just as Faust expected. He had cased the lakeside villa for weeks, studying the habits and comings and goings of the pampered occupants and their regular guests.

And now he was here to practice his specialty.

Faust was the anchor of the operation. He was the one who took the hostages, the one who took the greatest risks and the greatest pay.

Other members of Sinistra would hold the hostages until the ransom was to be collected. Then once again Faust would come into action for the final stage. Hand off the hostages or *hands off* the hostages. It was up to the family of the abductees. If they didn't follow the payment plans or proved treacherous in the negotiations, Faust would take the necessary measures. The pound of flesh.

The hostages would return home headless. That sort of thing spoke the loudest in this business. A man like Faust couldn't afford failure. It was either money or murder. Nothing in between.

Murder no longer bothered him. By now it was all just a numbers game. Some bodies had to fall to show that he was a serious man. He was a total professional whose profession more often than not included death.

"Now for the lady," Faust said, leading the way quietly out the back door to the rear of the villa where the sun-struck waters of Lake Como shone like a mirror.

"With pleasure."

"Not too much." Faust looked at his companion. "At least not until we see which way the operation goes. Then you will get whatever you deserve."

Donato nodded. Each man in the business had his own rewards. Some it was fortune. Some it was flesh.

Faust casually walked across the rolling green lawn in back of the villa. A cool breeze blew in from the lake, winding around the stone cupids sprouting from the primly cut grass and rippling the surface of a circular pond alive with streaming goldfish.

And farther down, close to the water, was a pair of lovebirds.

"Beautiful," Faust commented, studying them through the Ingram's sights. Then he nodded to Donato, the gesture setting the big man in discreet and dangerous motion.

The hunting party moved swiftly toward the lake, two-man teams sweeping down both sides of the villa to cut off any avenue of escape while Faust and Donato went straight down the middle.

The prey waited unaware, like fawns grazing in the grass while their stalkers closed in. The intruders moved with the authority and sureness that came from experience. This was nothing new for most of them.

They knew their jobs as well as they knew the land itself.

Like most resort areas in northern Italy's lake district, this was prime hunting ground for Sinistra and the other kidnapping rings the press had dubbed L'Anonima Sequestri, the anonymous kidnapping industry that had gained record profits during the past twelve months.

Close to the Swiss border and nestled in a year-long mild climate, Lake Como and Lake Maggiore were the havens of choice for the wise and wealthy elite from Milan, Italy's business capital.

Firs, pines and cypress groves followed the curves of the lakes, surrounding them with lush blankets of green. It was a European Eden with resorts, fishing villages and monasteries spread out along the shores.

It was also money in the bank or blood on the ground for the legions of kidnappers and killers who plied their trade in the area.

Most of the kidnap rings were based in southern Italy, siphoning ransoms from their wealthier brethren in the north.

But the high-profit underworld industry was not limited to the southern gangs. There were always new groups moving in, presenting a kaleidoscope of clandestine movements for the authorities to confront. Seasoned criminals, mercenaries and freelance terrorists banded together in ever-shifting alliances. Sometimes they broke up after a single hit or lasted for several abductions and ransoms. And sometimes they metamorphosed into something much bigger or deadlier than anyone imagined.

Such a group was Sinistra, one of the newest groups on the scene. In its relatively short existence, it had developed a brutal reputation. It had also gathered several fortunes while seeding the land with corpses.

They were the busiest outfit around, except perhaps for the undertakers.

HER SKIN WAS AS FLAWLESS as the white statues that stood guard on the green gardened terraces of Villa Condorri. And her figure was just as well sculpted, a figure that now baked in the afternoon sun glittering upon the mirror-smooth surface of Lake Como.

With a delicate peeling motion, she lowered the top of her untied red bikini, which had come straight from the showroom of the Condorri designer shop in Milan.

The motion wasn't lost on the man who sat beside her on a matching chaise longue, lifting his shades to drink in the view. Giancarlo Condorri had a dark Mediterranean complexion and a lean and well-oiled runner's body that glistened in the sun. He also had the smile of a man who resided in a boundless paradise whenever he wasn't learning the tricks of the fashion trade in his father's headquarters in nearby Milan.

The shore of the lake sat at their feet, a landscaped wall of trees guarding their privacy on both sides.

To help fend off the heat, a chilled bottle of wine from one of the family's Lombard vineyards sat between them. Soaking in the sunlight and sipping chilled wine in a drowsy duet had become a regular thing for them.

Like Roman gentry of old, everything the world had to offer was theirs.

Beauty, pleasure, safety.

It was all part of the tradition. Knowing how to spend wealth was as important as knowing how to earn it. The couple on the grass would help that tradition to continue. It was understood by both families that eventually they would be married. Giancarlo Condorri was the heir apparent of one of Milan's

premier fashion houses, and Sylvia Magnus was the
daughter of a respected Milanese newspaper pub-
lisher whose empire had grown from a small fashion
weekly to a conglomerate of tabloids and daily papers and several magazines.

The fashion and media empires would also be
joined in wedlock when Giancarlo and Sylvia walked
down the aisle to the altar.

But that was sometime in the hazy future.

Right now all they had to do was bake in the sun.

A SHADOW BLOCKED THE SUN. Sylvia frowned, stirring from the half slumber she'd fallen into, and
opened her eyes. The man who owned the shadow
was tall and lean, dressed in a dark suit and wearing
a smile that held no warmth.

He was savoring the shock on her face.

Her panicked eyes picked out other forms moving
across the grounds, men with wicked-looking weapons heading toward the boat house where one of the
mechanics was working on the cruiser's engine.

She looked to her left and saw Giancarlo freezing
like a block of ice, his impulse of jumping to his feet
short-circuited by the sight of the weaponry arrayed
against them.

But there was something else at work in Giancarlo, a trait ingrained in him since youth—never
turn away from trouble; always face it.

He faced it now, pushing himself up from the ground and leaping toward the man with the silenced weapon.

Like a man disciplining an unruly pet, Faust's hands flew straight out, breaking Giancarlo's intended choke hold and pushing his hands harmlessly away.

Almost as an afterthought he rammed the pistol grip of the Ingram onto Giancarlo's head.

There was a sickening, cracking sound, and the young man of wealth dropped to his knees.

Faust's pointed shoe lashed out in a blur and kicked Giancarlo in the ribs, toppling him over onto the grass. The young man tried to crawl back to his feet, but then the nausea caught up to him and swept away his hold on consciousness. He sprawled out face-forward into the soft earth.

"That's better." Faust waved the Ingram toward the frightened, pampered blonde, slicing the barrel through the air like a conductor orchestrating her fear.

"You have no similar inclination?" he asked. "You want to try to show your wrath?"

Sylvia bit her lip. It was so disorienting. The man was brutal, but he was so polite. And he wore a mask of tender concern. All part of his toying with her.

"Well?" he insisted. "Answer me."

"No. I don't want to try anything." She spoke like an automaton, carefully choosing a neutral tone. But her body shook in an uncontrollable shiver, giving away the fear that raged through her.

He nodded. "Good. Then I think you and I will get along fine. You see, Sylvia, you are coming with me."

She looked straight at the gun, the cold metal eye that gazed back at her with an ugly truth. She had no say in the matter, nor did the unconscious Giancarlo. That had been made too clear.

And she knew no help would come from Galantine. Whatever help he could give had already been offered and had been taken and crushed by this man.

Sylvia straightened her bikini top, then said, "Let me get some more clothes."

"No. That won't be necessary. We'll take care of all of your needs."

"What do you mean?" she asked.

The hulk in the suit stepped up beside the man with the gun, his eyes direct. No sophisticated games with this one. Just brute force and desire.

"I want your complete cooperation, Sylvia," Faust replied. "From now on you ask no questions. You do what I say. And if all goes well, then you and your playmate will play once again. If not, then a rather more undesirable fate awaits you."

She heard voices from the boat house. The mechanic was shouting at the intruders.

Several sputtering, popping sounds drifted up from the water. Then the mechanic spoke no more, and the soft cough of the cruiser's engines stopped.

The silence that followed was broken by the heavy footsteps of two more intruders running up the dock, moving toward them.

Another pair of gunmen approached from the other side of the estate. They exchanged glances with the sleek gunman who was obviously in charge.

He blessed her again with his demonic smile and slipped off his jacket. The man's short-sleeve shirt exposed lean muscular arms with veins running through them like iron coils. It made her think of a cat who'd shown its claws. If anything, this man was more dangerous than he first appeared. His body was forged from the same metal as his will.

"Here," he said, tossing the jacket to her. "Wear this for now and come with us."

The other men grabbed Giancarlo under the arms and propped him to his feet. A hideous blue-gray bruise had blossomed on the side of his head, and he doubled over from the stabbing pain in his ribs.

Giancarlo stood there on wobbly feet, his eyes blinking from the sun as he tried to figure out what insane world he was coming back to.

"Words of advice," Faust advised him. "Don't think. Don't talk. Just do whatever we say. Understand?"

Giancarlo groaned.

"I'm *asking* if you understand me."

"Yes," Giancarlo gasped.

"Good. Let us go, then. Make it look as if we are all friends. We walk out the front door nice and slow, get into the car and drive away. Then you will live happily ever after... or you will die for a very long time."

Faust looked around one more time. There were no boats close enough to see what was going on in the secluded villa, no swimmers, no fishermen.

He looked up suddenly as a cloud passed overhead and a shadow lurched forward, the Ingram automatically swinging in its direction. Then he laughed. The shadow belonged to a stone cupid.

"No witnesses," Faust said, triggering a burst. Stone chips flew as the silenced 9 mm rounds chopped off the neck of the cupid. The head fell to the ground with a heavy thud, then rolled down to his feet. "Looks like love is out of season."

The parade of gunmen and victims moved back toward the villa. Once inside they swept through it like a breeze, pausing only at a large antique table in the hallway that gleamed and shone with the care of ages.

Faust slipped on a pair of thin driving gloves, then nodded at Donato who removed a thin minicassette player from his pocket. In his beefy hand it looked like a toy from a dollhouse. Donato handed it to Faust.

The Sinistra specialist pressed the soft-touch button that eased the cassette well open and made sure it was loaded with the tape he'd prepared.

"You installed new batteries?" Faust asked.

Donato nodded.

"Good. On such things empires rise or fall. At least in this empire."

He played the tape once, smiling as he listened to the short and precise message. It sounded like carefully orchestrated music to him, an untraceable symphony of ransom demands. The words were spliced together from snippets of recorded newscasts.

It they did trace the message, it would be a host of news anchors, making news instead of reporting it.

Faust rewound the message, then placed the player on the table, carefully avoiding any scratches on the polished surface.

After all, he wouldn't want them to think he was inconsiderate.

The Alitalia commercial jet from Rome to Milan touched down at Linate airport early in the morning, carrying several businessmen in pin-striped suits and an Executioner in a black Windbreaker and jeans.

Mack Bolan was traveling as a tourist under the name Mike Belasko, and he was there to see the sights.

Especially Lake Como.

After lingering over a cup of black coffee at the airport long enough to see if anyone was watching him with too much interest, Bolan went out to the parking lot where a dark green Fiat was waiting for him.

With a casual glance around the parking lot, Bolan took out the slim key that had been given to him at the U.S. Embassy in Rome. He unlocked the door on the driver's side and slipped his tall frame into the compact car, levering the seat all the way back.

Then he made a quick check of the vehicle. It had everything he needed, including an emergency survival kit complete with aspirin, bandages, ointment and a Heckler & Koch P-7 squeeze-cocker automatic pistol, which would see him through any rough traffic he met on the five-mile ride into Milan. Once there an arsenal awaited him, courtesy of another "tourist" who happened to be spending some time in Milan—Hal Brognola, Justice Department honcho and director of its Sensitive Operations Group.

Brognola was one of the few true friends Bolan had, and the men shared a mutuál respect for each other. When the big Fed put out a call for the Executioner, he knew the warrior would respond.

Right now the call was loud and clear.

Bolan had already heard about the kidnap through the media. Soon he would hear the real story.

He shifted the Fiat into gear and drove toward Milan, passing swiftly through the outer rings of sprawling factories, then slowing as he neared the shining city itself, a maze of old-world monuments and flashy high-tech headquarters of banking and engineering firms.

It was crowded.

It was slow.

And though he met his share of homicidal drivers, no one was out to kill him for real. So far the spook precautions seemed to be holding up well.

No leaks. No hits. No errors.

But that could change at any moment.

It had been a while since Bolan had been in Milan, but it all came back to him quickly. The pattern of the city was etched into his brain from previous operations.

The rendezvous was set at an ornate row of apartment houses maintained by the U.S. consulate as an adjunct to their official presence on Piazza della Repubblica, a not-so-covert base for undercover operations.

The apartment complex was within walking distance of the consulate, close enough to shuffle people back and forth but faraway enough to maintain anonymity.

Most of the people who stayed at the complex were high-class transients, businessmen with government ties, spies at every level of government, military men, an occasional defector or two, legitimate arms brokers and visiting politicians. To avoid entrapment from foreign services while in Milan, the visitors were provided a secure place to stay that was out of the public and private eye. If anyone was going to do the entrapping, it would be the seldom-seen landlords of the complex.

Despite the old-world ambience of colored glass and cut stone, a brace of surveillance cameras steadily monitored the area inside and out. Most of the windows and doors were equipped with a variety of anti-intrusion devices and sensors.

Many of the rooms were off-limits to all but a chosen few, always kept ready for hush-hush meetings between American and Italian spy services.

A slow-moving moat of plainclothes security men surrounded the complex, apparently just passing time by reading newspapers in parked cars or walking past the glamorous facades like tourists who had an overwhelming interest in baroque architecture.

The ring of security made sure that people who didn't belong never got past the front door.

Mack Bolan belonged.

The security people who ushered him through the side entrance knew him as Mike Belasko, although to these people names were never fast and hard.

A few key words were exchanged, cementing the fact that Bolan was Belasko—at least on paper—and then he was escorted down a high-ceilinged hallway that led to the inner sanctum where a warren of rooms spilled off to the sides.

Leaving his escort behind, the warrior avoided the ancient elevator and took the wide curving stairwell up to the fourth floor conference room, which had been swept recently for bugs.

He crossed the threshold and strode directly to a man who was standing by the windows. As he shook the big Fed's hand, the warrior said, "Let's have it, Hal. I hear there's no time to waste."

"You've got that right, Striker. Take a seat." Brognola wheeled to the table a video deck with three different slots, which would accommodate U.S. and international tape formats. He held a videotape in his hand with the word Sinistra written on the label. He loaded the tape into the deck. A moment later a rough-cut documentary flashed on the large monitor on top of the deck. It was a very private documentary, made up of surveillance shots, mug shots and dossiers of the prime players in Italy's kidnap industry. Decades old, the industry came and went just like many of the other legitimate businesses. And so did the faces.

The practitioners ranged from hard-core extremist groups to common criminals posing as political extremists to lend a crooked kind of respectability to their actions. Now and then a handful of mercenaries or ex-spooks went into the business for one-shot deals and stayed in longer, tempted by the easy money and fast living.

There was never any shortage of criminals eager to make a killing in the kidnap game.

"Recently a number of organized kidnap and kill teams from the south of Italy have garnered a lot of attention in the national media," Brognola said as the tape showed a number of mountain strongholds, followed by faces of kidnap victims—both dead and alive.

"Collectively the kidnap gangs are known as L'Anonima Sequestri. But the gangs aren't as anonymous as the name implies. Italian police and security organizations have publicly traced nearly half of the abduction and ransom operations in the past twenty years to the 'Ndrangheta organization, based mainly in Calabria. But there are also several long-established Mafia clans and a lot of new groups moving into the industry. Poverty breeds crime, according to the experts, and since the south is the poorest part of the country, many of the groups come from there.''

"Crime breeds crime," Bolan interjected. "It's poverty of character we're dealing with here. The choice they make has little to do with money. You and I both know the Italian government has poured billions of dollars into the so-called poverty-stricken regions. And most of that money has been swallowed up by the underworld along with the money that comes from their rackets.''

"You've been doing your homework.''

"Just keeping up.''

The tape showed Villa Condorri at Lake Como exactly as the police discovered it—the body of Alfredo Galantine in the hallway, the debris of the statue in the back of the villa and the corpse of the mechanic.

"Sometimes a group of small-timers will pose as members of one of the bigger clans when they make a hit. That's to put fear into their victims and speed the ransom along. But other times, the newer group wants to make a name for itself. I think that's what we're dealing with here.'' Brognola paused the videotape and reached inside his shirt pocket. "Especially with this. Give it a listen.''

The big Fed placed the pocket-size recorder in the center of the table and played a high-quality duplicate of the microcassette tape left by the kidnappers.

A bizarre sequence of different voices all spliced into one continuous message filled the room. It was an eerie sensation to hear the succession of speakers, most of them with strong eloquent voices, while they delivered an inhuman message for the kidnappers.

It was a demand for total cooperation from the families of the abductees and an order not to involve any of the hostage rescue teams the government always had on hand. The kidnappers claimed to have connections inside Italy's elite special intervention squads and would know if any of them were involved. The listeners also were to start getting together the money so it would be ready when the time came to hand it over.

"It's not the message that clued us in to their identity," Brognola said. "It's the medium. The spliced tape. Whoever put that together spent a lot of time selecting just the right word. You'll notice the message is extremely polite and gracious, as if the kidnapper wanted to be taken as a gentleman—an equal to the victims he's attacked."

"That's still not a signature unless—"

"Unless other abductions involved the same kind of tape," Brognola interrupted, nodding as he snapped the eject button and popped out the small tape. "Same kind of personality. That's exactly what we've got right here. The same kind of tape used on their greatest hits. The nature of the tapes has been kept out of the media so far. There've been several previous kidnappings all with the same MO—quick and brutal execution of the abduction, murder as a matter of course, any bystanders or security men who happen to be around get whacked without a second thought, a clean getaway and the spliced tape."

"Who's behind it?" Bolan asked.

"Sinistra."

"Which is?"

"It means 'left.' "

"You known I speak the language, Hal. I know what the word means. But how does the group use the name? Is it a genuine leftist organization? Or just a bunch of psychopaths masquerading under a political cloak?"

"Cloak, pure and simple," Brognola replied. "Though they dumped some money on a few charities, it was only a fraction of the money they've taken in. And they fed the usual crap to the media, saying it's all in the name of the people, and the money will be distributed to the needy masses."

"Maybe it's time we added some dagger to the cloak."

"Long past time."

Bolan nodded as the big Fed continued the briefing with the videotape. He knew the pattern. They had to move fast or the group would grow too strong and well organized to be put out of business. They already had safe houses, specialists, and now were claiming their territory. Unless the head was severed now, the body would grow, bloated on money, fear and violence until it became just like all the other organized crime networks.

Brognola paused the videotape again when a photograph of a young woman appeared on the screen. "This is Sylvia Magnus, one of the kidnap victims."

"Beautiful," Bolan said. "Too beautiful."

"Exactly. None of these groups has any sterling record when it comes to the safety of their female captives. What happens to them during captivity doesn't always make it to the papers."

Brognola moved on to the photograph of Sylvia Magnus's fiancé.

"Who was the main target?" Bolan asked.

"We don't know yet. It could have been either of them, and the other was just a target of opportunity. Or it could have been planned from the beginning to snatch the two of them. Both families have wealth. Both wield considerable influence in the culture of Milan as well as the international scene. With all of their holdings, they're well past the hundred-million mark."

"Which brings us to the big question," Bolan said. "Why am I here? More to the point, Hal, why are *you* here? The Italians have their own people to deal with this kind of thing. This is their turf. And though

I'm willing to strike at Sinistra, I'd like to know more.''

''Understood. This is where the possibilities can get a bit more unsettling.''

''Shoot.''

''Corbin Magnus, the father of the abducted girl, is more than just a media giant,'' Brognola told him. ''In fact his media empire was just a fluke that grew out of a cover he built for himself back when he was active in the Italian security services.''

''I suspected one or the other family had some heavy connections.''

''They don't come any heavier than Corbin Magnus,'' the big Fed stated, fast-forwarding the tape to a shot of a silver-haired man stepping out of a limousine in the courtyard of his Milan headquarters.

Corbin Magnus was taller than the bodyguards who surrounded him, and he was built like a heavyweight boxer. The man's clothes were immaculate.

''Magnus was one of the key players in the rescue of General Dozier,'' Brognola said. ''He was at the center of the hurricane back then, and he came out of it without a single hair out of place.''

Bolan nodded. The Dozier case was one of the most successful joint Italian-American operations to date. Although the U.S. provided its own Special Forces teams to help in the search for the American general abducted by the Red Brigades, the Italian special units carried out most of the actual assaults on suspected safe houses where it was believed General Dozier was held. After all, it was their turf.

Perhaps more important than the elite units sent in by the U.S. was the topflight, black-flight communications teams they sent to Italy. America's little-known Intelligence Support Activity ferried in U.S. helicopters and surveillance vans that intercepted the supposedly secure radio communications used by the Brigades.

Picking up a web of clandestine communications across Vicenza, Padua, Florence and Rome, the Italian authorities were able to expose Red Brigades and Mafia activity throughout the country. This treasure trove of information, leads and locations helped the Italian services crack terrorist and organized crime cells for the next few years.

"Magnus was working with GIS at the time," Brognola said, "commanding most of the operations in the north of Italy."

Groupe Interventional Speciali was the paramilitary branch of the Carabinieri, an elite core of commando, police and intelligence operatives. They were the ones who combed the countryside by the thousands in the search, coordinating the activities of the various covert cadres.

"He also helped crack the P2 Affair."

That brought Magnus up another notch in Bolan's estimation. The P2 Affair had almost plunged Italy into a state of anarchy, bringing an underground government a step away from ultimate power. P2 was an unofficial off-the-books power structure composed of police, military and intelligence officers, along with high-ranking confederates in the international banking system. P2 had established links with both Western and Eastern Bloc security services and was well on its way to becoming an independent state.

The whole affair became unraveled only when a number of Italian security chiefs risked their careers and lives to bring the scandal into the open.

P2 fell, and bit by bit the covert services removed the reins of power from the clandestine rogue elephant that had been trampling over the legitimate government officials.

"We barely escaped that train wreck ourselves," Brognola said. "Magnus helped expose a lot of bad apples among U.S. operatives who'd been co-opted. That helped us contain a lot of runaway operations that otherwise would have succeeded, and who knows what damage they might have done."

"So you and Magnus go way back," Bolan said.

"We've worked together on a lot of similar operations. We owe each other a lot of favors, and sometimes we don't have any choice but to collect. Magnus turned to me on this one."

The Executioner sat back for the rest of the briefing. If Magnus didn't feel free to move on his own, at least not yet, it meant that there were a lot of wild cards in the game. To improve his hand when the time came, Bolan paid strict attention as Brognola fed him background on the Italian operative.

Magnus was currently "retired." Like many in the intelligence field, he still kept a hand in, helping whenever he was called upon. His cover of a media magnate had come true a lot quicker than anyone imagined. Magnus had a talent for ferreting out information and packaging it in a way that struck the fancy of the public. Not unusual for a man in the covert field.

To avoid any potential conflict of interest, he'd turned his operations over to the Italian government, then started over from scratch. By then he had a name, and he had expertise. His new enterprises rocketed to the top even faster than before.

And so a real media empire was born.

Brognola turned to the other wild card in the deck—Condorri. The elder Condorri was in a similar position of power, but his was strictly business. There was no lifetime of gray operations that had to be covered up.

And though Condorri appeared to be well-off on paper, Bolan knew that would be checked out.

What if the fashion designer's empire was starting to crumble and he needed money? What if he arranged a collaboration with friends in Sinistra and the deal went bad? It was too morbid to dwell on, although it was a distant possibility. But even so it would be examined just like everything else in this case.

Brognola presented a brief summary of the media coverage of the kidnapping. The murder of the Condorri bodyguard and the abduction of heir and heiress was discovered by a servant returning to the villa, who immediately notified the police. The mechanic's body was discovered in the boat house and the details of the snatch were worked out.

Word leaked to the papers immediately, probably from someone connected to either of the prominent families.

And then the kidnappers played out the first stage. They waited for the inevitable police search, then sent another tape warning to both Magnus and Condorri not to cooperate further with the authorities. Sinistra was calling all the shots.

"That's another reason why you're here," Brognola said. "We still can't be sure if the Sinistra boast about having connections in the Carabinieri is true or not. Maybe they can detect if the paramilitary groups are launching a strike. Maybe it's all smoke. At this point Magnus isn't taking a chance. He wants an outside force working on it, a third party that can't be tied to him."

"I kind of figured that," Bolan replied. "I think we can work something out that'll lend us deniability. Like we did in the old days." In his wars against the Mafia in America a key strategy for winning—hell, for surviving—involved pitting one crime Family against another. In a brotherhood that expected feuds and ambushes and was always ready to war to the last man, anonymous attacks were almost as regular as the rain.

And now, sitting here in Milan, a black-clad weatherman was predicting a heavy-metal storm.

Bolan turned his attention to the videotape, memorizing the procession of masked faces that came onscreen, the new breed of sleek-coated predators. Most of them dressed well and acted well, but their true natures were impossible to hide. It was evident in the eyes. They looked on society as a world to be harvested, a world vulnerable to reapers like themselves.

"Chief on the list is Amory Faust," Brognola said, as the screen showed a number of police sketches gathered from those rare witnesses who survived encounters with him. "At least that's the name that's floating around. No such name on record. He changes his appearance frequently and considers killing a way of life. He stays constantly on the move, although the Italians have a line on some of his contacts, some of the small-time goons connected to Sinistra."

"You think it's Faust?" Bolan asked.

"Hard to say. This operation has his marking on it and it could very well be him. Or it could be an admirer, a copycat killer. Our counterparts believe that a number of different terrorists may be enhancing his legend by operating under the name of Faust. But whether it's Faust or some other Sinistra soldier, we still don't know if he's aware of the true nature of his prize. Was this a deliberate grab because of Magnus's covert past, or was it just because he was a good target?''

"Dead is dead, whatever the reason," Bolan said.

"No argument there. But if they find out who Magnus is—or was—this can lead to a lot more misery. They'll go to any lengths to work on the girl if they think they can pry some damning intelligence from Magnus. Striker, it's up to us.''

2

The morning air sliced through the cracks in the wooden shed like knives, the chill jabbing at every inch of Sylvia Magnus's skin. She wrapped the silk jacket tighter around her shoulders, the one given to her by her abductor. Though she hated the touch of the garment, her body cried out for warmth. Aside from the two-piece swimsuit she'd been wearing on the day the killers took her from Villa Condorri, the jacket was the only piece of clothing they'd given her.

The bastards.

She stretched out on the damp floor. Her muscles were cold and tight, and her bones were stiff and brittle from the hard wood she'd slept on. Her prison was a crib, a manger. It was a stall fit for livestock.

Did they select it for her to teach her a lesson? she wondered. Was this punishment for the idle life she led as a wealthy heiress? Or was it coincidence?

No, she thought. Amory Faust left nothing to coincidence.

This, too, was part of his choreographed capture—the sudden appearance on the lakeside paradise, the casual murder of two men from the Condorri household and his feigned politeness. It was all a game to him. Even this jacket, she thought. He wanted her to have his scent wrapped around her, his perfumed lethal scent.

And he wanted her to have his name.

Amory Faust.

He made sure she heard it several times from his men. He even said it out loud to her more than once, seeming to enjoy the sound it made, as if "Amory Faust" was a favorite song to be played over and over.

Only two alternatives came to mind about why he was so careless of his identity. It either didn't matter that she knew his name because he planned on killing her after she provided sport for the troops—a dark future he had hinted at several times in his polite but oblique manner—or his name was as empty and transient as the sweet dreams of freedom she tasted in her sleep night after night.

Amory Faust, a favorite song. Amory Faust, an anthem of hate, a murderer's marching song.

"No!" she suddenly shouted.

She slipped off the jacket and snapped it like a whip. The arms flailed in the air before the expensive cloth dropped onto the floor. Dust and debris flew in the air from the rotting floor, then swept into her lungs.

Sylvia coughed, then grabbed her throat and retched, the swimsuit blonde reduced to a sweat-soaked captive, her matted hair a crown of thorns.

She screamed.

It was loud and shrill and made her feel better, if only for a fleeting moment. Anger was the burning light of the soul. Anger would see her through.

Anger and hope.

She rubbed her hands up and down her arms, stirring up the blood and chasing away the cold. Slowly she uncoiled her body and stretched out flat on the floor. Her toes extended all the way like a swimmer about to dive. Her calf muscles tightened, her buttocks, her back, her shoulders, all tensed and stretched. Then came the release. She sighed, exhaling all the poison, all the tension, all the fear out of her body.

Then Sylvia took a long slow breath, inhaling it down to the pit of her abdomen, down to her soul itself, her bare back ignoring the splinters and grit on the floor.

If she was going to survive this captivity, if she was going to come out of this cage without being turned into a madwoman, she had to take control of her body and her mind.

After all, she was her father's daughter, and a Magnus never gave in, never yielded the only prize that mattered in the end. Her will. Her mind.

These were the lessons her father taught, lessons she thought were abstract sayings suitable to someone in his line of work. Though he'd never really explained what it was that he used to do, Sylvia had picked up enough hints over the years. She'd seen an endless procession of men in gray suits come to her house, men with no last names and men with no concrete occupations but with killing eyes.

She knew he was in the clandestine trade back then. What division, she wasn't sure. How long he was in it, or even if he was still in it, were questions she had no answers to.

And that brought one searing question to mind. Was this why they'd taken her? To get at him through her?

The chill came back.

She forced it from her mind, breathed it out. He would come for her, she thought. Or he would send someone after her. These men would pay. Amory Faust would lose a lot more than his phony name when he was through with her.

Her father would come for her. He would come. He would take her out of this hole. She said it over and over in her mind, a mantra that built up the ladder of hope once again.

She fell into an almost trancelike state, meditation and yoga slowly calming her down.

As morning wore on, the chill went away.

Then came the sun, which was almost as bad. First there was a temperate moment when the air in the shed lost its coldness. But then the heat grew stronger, baking down on the dried wood. And then the suffering started again.

The stifling air and the endless echo of fear that was never far from the surface turned this tiny little cage into her own private patch of hell.

She was in the mountains somewhere, she thought. Mountains that she'd known since she was a child. In the mountains the cool caress of Alpine winds chased away the heat of the day, but then as night dragged on, ice crept into the air.

She was close to home, maybe near the Swiss border. Maybe near one of the lakes, one of the resorts she and her family vacationed on when she was young, a time when she knew nothing of the world. Nothing of the evil practiced by men like Amory Faust.

Sylvia pounded on the wooden slats suddenly, her fist thudding into the wall until the heel of her palm was bruised. She heard shouting from outside, shouting and heavy footsteps on the dirt.

There was a rattling outside the door, a thunking and sliding sound as the bar slid free. A wall of light blinded her as the hinged door sprang open, then the sun was blacked out by the huge bearded figure that stepped into the shed.

"What do you want?" It was that voice again, the guttural, primitive voice. Uneducated. Unfeeling. Unthinking.

The blocked-out sun made the gruff-voiced thug seem even larger than he was.

And though his face wore a mask of anger, his eyes had a different emotion entirely. "Whatever you want," he said, "I can give you. You know that, girl." He laughed, then, a mad little hawklike screech.

She fell silent and scuttled across the floor, a frightened thing, a mouse, an insect, a creature on the run. As her eyes got used to the light, she saw that this was the same man who'd silenced Giancarlo two days earlier.

He, too, was being kept at the mountain hideout, perhaps in a crib just like this. His spirit had come back to him after she called out to him from her wooden cage. He'd made his demands, then, trying to throw his weight around—until this door-filling gunman pounded it out of him.

It didn't take long. Some shouts. Some thuds. Some cracking of boards, maybe of bones. And then Giancarlo was silent once again, except for a few groans.

Sylvia gave up all hope of talking to Giancarlo again. The next time she tried it, they might come after her. They might not kill her, she thought, but they could hurt her.

It was all part of her prisoner status.

Amory Faust had promised that she would be left alone, unmolested as long as she gave them no trouble. But if she tried anything, she'd be at the mercy of the guards.

"What do you want?" the guard asked again, taking a step toward her, backing her against the wall.

"Nothing."

"Too bad." He laughed once more, an idiotic bray that painted the enclosed room with fear.

Then he stepped back out and slammed the door behind him, locking and barring it.

His mouth pressed against the crack in the door, he said, "Let me know when you need it."

3

The man in black kept to the shadows of the medieval village that crowned the Lombard hilltop, walking unhurriedly along the tall stone terraces that held well-kept gardens in place.

Despite the cobblestone road that wound snakelike through Monte Cappelli, it wasn't entirely an ancient place. To survive the departure of many of the younger people who went off to find work in Milan and its ring of factory-rich suburbs, part of the town had become an "old-fashioned" resort.

A tavern in the shape of a blockhouse sprang up at the southern edge of town, the beams carefully treated to look old and weathered. And next to it was a two-story café and restaurant, reminiscent of days gone by. That, too, had been built within the past ten years.

It was pretty much the same throughout the area the locals called the new quarter. The clubs, restaurants and inns that catered to the faster, moneyed crowd had succeeded in bringing notice to Monte Cappelli once more.

Very quaint, Mack Bolan thought, as he took up position in a patch of woods across the road from the torch-lit tavern in medieval disguise.

Wrapped in the shadows of the dark green boughs, the Executioner reached into his black nylon gear bag and threaded the sound suppressor onto the Beretta 93-R.

Just in case.

He didn't plan on reducing the population of Monte Cappelli any more than he had to this night, but sometimes plans didn't work out. With a 15-round clip of 9 mm Parabellums and the selector set to 3-round burst, he was ready to move against all comers if it came down to a firefight.

The way it went down would be up to his target, Felix Giamante, who was due any moment now. This was usually the first round on his roadside rambling. Most of the time he was alone, but sometimes he brought his hardmen with him.

Giamante had been drawn to the nightlife like a moth to the flame. According to the dossier Bolan had been provided, the man was an all-around hell-raiser—hard liver, hard player, hard killer, hard drinker. Ever since he burst onto the scene a few years earlier, his prosperity had grown by leaps and bounds. Coincidentally his fortune rose almost in direct proportion to the rash of kidnappings that plagued the surrounding area.

He'd built a splendid villa close to the rocky spire that had given Monte Cappelli its name in the distant past. But the only thing Giamante worshiped was money, and he was hell-bent on spending it just as fast as he made it.

His kind wouldn't live long enough to retire. There were too many hazards in his line of work. And one of them, a tall lean figure in black, was ready to step in his way.

Bolan didn't have long to wait. A flashy red Ferrari careered around the corner, engine roaring, tires screeching.

Giamante parked the vehicle directly across from the tavern.

Less than twenty yards away from the fate that was finally catching up to him, he locked the car, pocketed the key and headed for the dim lights and bright music.

LIKE A PRINCELING of old, Felix Giamante strode into the tavern, loudly pushing the door back against the wall and holding it there for a moment like an unfurled wing while his hawklike gaze played over the crowd.

He sauntered over to a high-backed booth at the rear of the tavern, smiling up at the dark-haired waitress who glided over to his table, a resigned look on her face.

"What will you have tonight?" she asked.

"You."

"To drink."

"I'm happy just drinking in your beauty," Giamante replied. "But a bottle of wine would be nice, too."

She laughed, falsely and with a bit of fear in her voice. A quality he liked in his women.

When his hand shivered up the back of her stockinged thigh, the women's smile only froze. It didn't break.

It wasn't smart to have a man like Felix Giamante angry at you. He was the kind of man who took offense, the kind who made threats and carried them out.

While she fetched the wine, Giamante stretched his arms over the back of the booth, "accidentally" displaying his holster.

Beneath his expensive suit he carried an expensive gun. It was a SIG P-210-2. The sleek-finished Swiss automatic could fire 9 mm or 7.65 mm Parabellum rounds. Right now the barrel and clip were set for 9 mm loads. The bigger, the better, he thought, holding the pose as his waitress returned.

She saw the weapon but pretended not to.

He smiled. To some women a weapon like that was an aphrodisiac. Not that it mattered. He didn't have to waste much time courting any of them. They knew who he was and that to spurn his affections could bring down a plague upon their houses.

One of these days he would take her, he thought, watching the sweep of her hips as she departed.

But this was only the first stop.

There would be other places tonight. Other women.

GIAMANTE LEFT THE TAVERN a half hour later, his step heavier, his heart lighter, wine coursing through his veins. He was well on the way to a world-class drunk.

He suddenly stopped midway across the road. There was something in the air, a scent of danger, something not right.

He laughed, dismissing it. What couldn't be right in the world of Felix Giamante? He wasn't a child afraid of the dark. The dark was his home, his arena.

He crouched, fumbling slightly with the keys as he unlocked the Ferrari. Just as the lock jumped free, he felt the stab of lightning and everything went white.

A jolt of electricity shot clear to his toes. He thought of the thin blade sheathed inside his laquered boot and wondered if the lightning would sear its image into his flesh.

And then he realized it wasn't lightning.

His mind finally decoded the nova that had gone off in his brain. Someone had come behind him so fast he hadn't even seen him and smashed his head into the window glass. Quite professionally. He hadn't even had a chance to react.

The assailant had made a fatal mistake. Whoever dared confront Felix Giamante would have an eternity to regret it.

Some of his bravado vanished as he was roughly spun around. Falling toward the ground, he managed to say, "Who—" And then lightning struck again. This time it was a heel kick to the breastbone.

He gasped for breath like a fish yanked out of water, then slumped to the cobblestone road, glimpsing a man in black towering over him as he descended toward unconsciousness. Giamante was out before his face touched the stone-cold street.

BOLAN EASED the red sports car off the shoulder of the road, drove it over a carpet of needles and fallen branches, then reached over and shook his passenger awake. Giamante had been bound hand and foot with nylon cuffs, and lay doubled over in the front seat like a chained simian.

The hardman slowly came around, realizing that he couldn't move his hands or his legs and that he was a prisoner.

To make up for his immobility, the man's eyes moved quickly, darting from left to right as they took in the situation, as they studied the man in black.

His face was painted for combat, and a glitter of blue steel shone from his unblinking gaze.

The Executioner watched impassively as Giamante's face worked like a mime displaying all his emotions.

First there was anger, then shock and finally fear.

None of them worked on Bolan.

The Executioner switched off the ignition, removed the key, then opened the driver's door. He hefted his gear bag, acting as if Giamante weren't there, just part of the baggage to be disposed of when the time came.

"For God's sake, you bastard! Tell me what's going on! Damn, I have a right to know—"

Bolan waved the barrel of the Beretta toward Giamante, the shadow of the weapon marking a bull's-eye on his forehead. "You have a right to remain silent," he said. "A need actually. But you do have the right to die here and now. Care to exercise that right?"

The prisoner shook his head.

"All right. I'll tell you what's going on. Only because it serves my purpose. Understand?"

Giamante nodded.

"There's a war going on," the Executioner explained.

"With who?"

"Between your people and Sinistra."

"That's crazy! There's no war between our clans—"

"There is now," Bolan growled. "At least there will be. You and I are in the middle of a Sinistra stronghold. An enemy camp. Take a look around."

"I can't move that far," the bound gunman complained, craning his neck back and trying to look out at the countryside.

"A pity. I imagine a lot of your victims felt the same way. Tied up. Held hostage. Not knowing if they were going to be killed or released."

He let that sink in for a moment, let Giamante know that his career in the kidnap trade was an open book.

While Giamante mulled over his position, Bolan continued the show-and-tell. "Now if you *could* look around, you'd see a lot of woods. A lot of beautiful country. And if you looked real hard, you'd see the locusts."

The Executioner pointed the nose of the Beretta downhill, toward a cluster of white-walled buildings. "That's one of Sinistra's nests."

"*Sinistra?* I told you I have nothing to do with them. Who are you? Why are you doing this? There is plenty to go around for everyone. All of the Families can make money from the trade."

"That's why I'm doing it."

"But I have no quarrel with Sinistra. I don't know them. It's obvious there's been a mistake. I shouldn't be here. It's not fair—"

"That's life," Bolan told him. "Death, too. It never seems fair to anybody when the time comes. The hardmen down there will probably feel the same way."

Giamante started to curse, running out of talk, running out of hope. The pain from his bruised forehead reminded him what this man was capable of. He'd been taken down effortlessly, like a gnat brushed out of the way.

That knowledge painted a dim future for him. Shaking his head from side to side, Giamante looked at his captor's eyes. And still he saw ice there.

"I don't get it," he said. "If this is about the Magnus kidnapping, I'm innocent. I swear to you, I wasn't even here. I was—"

"You were in the south," Bolan replied. "On a holiday in Calabria, spending some of the ransom from your last job. Sharing the wealth with some of your friends."

"How do you know all this?"

"You are a closely watched man, Giamante."

The Executioner thought of the avalanche of intelligence Brognola had amassed from his Italian counterparts, who'd considered all of the likely candidates for the Magnus abduction. Giamante came out clean on this one. He'd been out of the area when the kidnappers struck. He'd also been under police surveillance as part of an operation tracking the links between the gangs in the north and south.

Giamante was innocent this time around, but there was enough dirt from his past, enough blood on his hands, to make him pay the price now.

"Whoever you are," the hardman said, "I'm sure you're reasonable. We can come to some kind of arrangement to avoid this . . . this war you speak of."

"No," the warrior replied, "I'm not a reasonable man. And there's no calling off the war." He nodded in the direction of the Sinistra stronghold. "In a little while some of those vermin are going to be exterminated."

"And me?"

"Good question," Bolan said. "You'll find out the answer when I get back."

THE AUTOMATIC RIFLE WAS top-flight, but not the man who wielded it. He was in his mid-twenties, tough and mean, but untrained when it came to dealing with professionals. Most of the time he held the Beretta BM 59 7.62 mm rifle like it was a metal-trimmed walking stick.

Bolan moved downhill from tree to tree in the spear of forest that flanked the Sinistra stronghold, looking but not looking at the sentry.

From past experience he knew that sometimes a man could sense when he was being stalked, almost as if the hairs on the back of his neck were antennae picking up the motion of an intruder. Bolan had been on the receiving end of that more than enough times to know it was true.

It was almost like a spectrum of death broadcasting in the night. If the stalker was too agitated, nerves bristling like static, there was always a chance the target would subconsciously pick up on it. The right approach was to move stealthily without focusing too hard on the target, but without losing sight, either.

The Executioner kept the man's silhouette on the edge of his vision as he angled toward him. He was moving on autopilot, letting his body do the thinking for him.

The Sinistra sentry was standing in the shadows, one foot on the wide slab of a freshly cut tree trunk, the other planted in the tall grass. Now and then he slapped, or blew a stream of cigarette smoke, at a cloud of gnats dizzily spinning around him. The glowing embers of his cigarette traced bright red scars in the night as it zapped around like a firefly.

The light would soon go out, Bolan thought as he edged closer, his camou-streaked face a shadowed mask, his breathing toned down to a soft and silent cadence.

The sentry suddenly gripped his rifle tighter, right hand moving toward the trigger.

He was at full attention now, ready for war.

Bolan steeled himself for the attack, wondering what had given him away. Whatever it was, his silent approach wouldn't be silent anymore. If the man turned around in the next few moments the Executioner would have to take him out fast with a burst from the Beretta 93-R. And from this distance the sentry might get off a shot or two of his own before he went down for good.

But then Bolan heard the same sound that had snapped the sentry out of his self-induced spell.

It was coming from the left, a searing rolling sound that drummed through the night, tires thrumming down the road, a steady clacking sound accompanying the whir of the tires. A loose fender or a piece of chrome was tapping against the chassis.

The sound carried far in the mountains.

Bolan relaxed. He hadn't been made yet.

The sentry was reacting to the wrong stimulus. His senses had told him something was wrong, and now the approaching car would dilute his suspicions.

Headlights sliced through the darkness as a twin beacon jagged up and down the winding road that cut through the ridges and wild forests of the Lombardy countryside. When the car drew near, the sentry darted several steps forward and craned his neck for a better look down the slope.

The Executioner picked up his pace while the rifleman was distracted.

The car drove by, its tires gradually whining out of earshot.

With the threat gone the sentry stood down, relieved that he wouldn't have to call out the troops. He backtracked to his former position by the tree stump.

Bolan was a lot closer now, almost close enough to take him without any of the others hearing a sound.

The cluster of houses was in a state of alert. A small army of soldiers waited inside, irregulars who'd learned their trade in the streets and the alleys. Leg breakers, head crushers, back-alley brutes who did the heavy work for Sinistra. And they hadn't come out to the countryside for a vacation.

The Sinistra hardmen had no knowledge of the intricate details of the kidnappings. They were a reserve force, ready to go into action when things got heavy. If the victims didn't carry out their part of the bargain, these men would carry out theirs.

Smoke coiled from a wood stove in the house nearest the sentry, just forty yards from where he stood guard. Muffled voices and the steady clink of bottles escaped from the rickety wood-frame windows. The scent of smoked meat drifted out into the night air, settling down like a haze around the house.

Off to the side of the clustered houses were penned-in goats and chickens. Everything the men needed to live on was provided for them in the hideaway. They could camp here in the countryside as long as they were needed.

Jagged clay driveways hewn out of the hillside led from the black ribbon of road up to a half-dozen pickups and cars parked close to the ramshackle front porches.

Not that anyone expected serious trouble.

The sentry was merely on duty in case one of the Sinistra higher-ups or the authorities came by.

If trouble did come, the men expected it to be in a parade of brightly lighted police cars, flashing lights and sirens and a horde of carabinieri asking questions, just as they'd been doing since the abductions. The police had been scouring the countryside, interrogating all suspects in the kidnapping trade.

A sudden burst of laughter from the house caught the sentry's attention. They were in there playing cards and drinking wine, making boasts. He shook his head. He should be in there with them. This was just a waste of—

A cold metal bar rapped against his temple, and he dropped to the ground.

Bolan stepped over the prostrate form and walked toward the lighted house.

MILO LOOKED at his watch when he heard the steps creaking on the wooden wraparound porch.

"Christ!" he said, slapping his cards down on the long trestle table and looking at the door. "Here he comes already. That bastard's never finished a full watch yet!"

"It's good for you, Milo," said the bald, bullet-headed man sitting across from him. Perhaps to make up for his baldness, Clement Lacazino sported a long rust-gray handlebar mustache that fell down the side of his mouth like fangs. "Good for us, too. With you out there, there'll be something left for us to drink later on."

"It's a crime," Milo stated. "A damn crime."

"Call the police," Lacazino suggested.

That brought a burst of laughter from the scarred men who sat around the table, supporting marble chins with thick palms and muscled slabs of forearm. Most of them had jack-o'-lantern smiles, teeth missing from long-ago brawls and never replaced.

Genuine laughter was rare among the crew. When it came, it was usually at Milo's expense. Since he made no secret of his scorn for guard duty, the others missed no opportunity to goad him about it. There were no prima donnas in this group. They all took the same risks and rewards. They all stood watch.

And now it was Milo's turn. He always followed Perry, and Perry always shaved time from his watch.

Milo shook his head as he gathered what was left of his stake across the splintered table. His wide, jowled face was red with anger, but it was just for show. In reality he welcomed the interruption. It was another bad hand, and he was losing too much to the other men gathered around the table.

"Go stand your watch, Milo," Lacazino told him. "Give us all a break."

The laughter covered up the approaching footsteps. Otherwise the hardmen might have noticed the heavier-than-usual steps.

There was a thump at the door, then a metallic sound as the latch clicked open and the door swung inward.

"Son of a bitch, Perry, you're early—"

Milo stopped in surprise when he saw Perry walking into the room, walking on dead man's legs.

The sentry pitched forward then, his head nodding wildly toward his breastbone as if he were controlled by puppet strings, staggering like a man full of wine. But he was full of eternity instead.

As the slain sentry's body crumpled to the floor, Milo reached for his weapon. Too late. Bolan stood in the doorway and opened with the Beretta 93-R.

He swept the table with 3-round bursts, the hushed sounds of the silenced pistol dropping Milo and two men on the left side of the table in an instant, their legs kicking in the air like insects hit with a poison cloud. But it was a 9 mm cloud, and it was moving all over the room.

All of them had been caught in that dead zone of surprise, still trying to register what happened to Perry even while the same thing was happening to them.

Bolan continued the sweep, the 9 mm Parabellum rounds eating into the wood table, skidding into bodies in a cloud of splinters. Chairs overturned, screams filled the air and blood ran on the floor like spilled wine.

Before the 15-round clip was empty, the warrior squeezed off several rounds from the SIG P-210-2. He stood his ground while a Sinistra gunman on the opposite side of the table scrambled for his shotgun.

It was a matter of time—the man was out of it and the Executioner controlled it.

He triggered a burst from the Swiss automatic pistol just as a shotgun blast tore a head-size hole in the door behind him.

It was the shotgunner's last act on earth as a brace of slugs propelled him into hell.

The Executioner followed up his initial bursts with calculated shots, moving to his right as another gunman opened up on him. The wraithlike man was firing long before he had sighted on his target.

Bolan stitched him with a burst that traveled up his chest and drilled into his skull. As the man tumbled over like a spouting fountain, the warrior zeroed in on the mustached hardman who'd jumped to his feet as soon as the Executioner had come in firing.

But the man was gone. He'd simply thrown himself backward through the side window, disappearing in a shower of glass and splintered wood.

At the same time Bolan heard sounds coming from one of the back rooms.

Footsteps pounded down an overhead hallway, approaching the staircase off to his left.

Suicide was just a few seconds away. If he stayed any longer, he'd stay forever.

Bolan emptied the Swiss pistol at the window where the huge man had escaped, firing a couple of rounds through the wall on both sides of the window. Then he dropped an ear-bursting concussion grenade in the middle of the room.

It exploded just as the reinforcements ran into the room, right into a nova blast. The magnesium stun grenade whited out all sound, leaving the hardmen in a state of shock.

The Executioner had backpedaled out the door, spun around and jumped. He landed in the grass, rolled, scrambled and dived for the side of a pickup truck.

Shouting erupted from the next house over, another beat-up barracks maintained by the Sinistra reserves. Hardcases raced out to join in the battle—and ran face-first into an inferno.

The Claymores that Bolan rigged by the front door sent a murderous hail of steel slicing through wooden walls like paper, through flesh like water. The deafening roar howled up the hillside, echoing from peak to peak.

And the screams of the Sinistra soldiers filled the night.

Bolan dashed back uphill toward the woods.

Wounded men poured out of the house like hornets, followed by armed men who'd survived the blast untouched. Together they staggered around in the darkness, screaming, firing automatic weapons at shadows.

The warrior led them on, stopping at the edge of the woods to fire a burst from his 93-R.

The sound attracted their attention, and like the children of Hamelin they followed him into the woods.

4

The hunters ran wild in the woods.

Feet snagging on tendrillike vines, skidding on dead bleached tree limbs, they surged through the dark forest. Branches slashed like whips into their faces.

Lacazino urged them on, raging like an ox as he punctuated his commands with thunderclap bursts from a cut-down shotgun to clear the way in front of him.

This was Lacazino's crew. He was the main contact with the Sinistra hierarchy. What happened tonight landed on his head. Unless he took control now and took revenge, his own people would come down on him.

While the shotgun loads stung into the woods and ripped through bark and leaves, the other men joined in the hot pursuit, fiery bursts stitching the darkness.

But none of them knew what they were shooting at—until it was too late.

Bolan had angled off to the side, letting them pass before he hit them again, using the roar of their automatic rifles to cover the silenced bursts from the Beretta 93-R. He had the wire stock unfolded now, and was taking careful aim.

One gunman stood on his toes, fatally surprised by the volley of 9 mm rounds that so quietly blew him away.

The man closest to him called out urgently.

Bolan answered with another burst, the silenced rounds ripping into tree trunks, then into flesh and bone.

The Executioner dropped back into the deep cover of the woods as the Sinistra crew realized what was happening, attracted by the muzzle-flashes of the Beretta or the crash of their fellow gunmen as they dropped dead to the ground.

"Over there!" Lacazino shouted, pointing the shotgun barrel at the cluster of trees that had been the Executioner's position. Like a wounded bear he led the way, firing two rounds from the shotgun. But by then Bolan was gone.

A half-dozen Sinistra soldiers followed Lacazino's lead and emptied their automatic rifles in the same direction. They crept closer and shredded the forest with heavy lead bursts.

Then the firing stopped.

They stepped through the undergrowth and scoured the site, barrels nosing in front of them. But there was no sign of the man who'd coolly walked into the middle of their stronghold and tried to mow them down.

The first two men on the scene had expected to find a bullet-riddled corpse. They continued their ghoulish treasure hunt, poking under bushes and kicking over stands of fallen trees while the rest of the hunters covered them.

"There's no one here," the first man said.

"Gone," his companion agreed. "Like a ghost."

Lacazino stepped forward, roughly pushing them out of the way. "There's no ghosts out here, you superstitious idiots!" he shouted. "Not *yet* anyway. But there will be by the time the night is over. Either him or us." He glared at the Sinistra soldiers, their faces colored with their fear of him.

And fear of the ghostly assassin.

"Take him," Lacazino ordered.

They moved into the woods, slower this time, fanning out and calling to one another while they closed in on their prey.

ECHOES OF WAR DRIFTED uphill to Felix Giamante. Exhausted from trying to escape imprisonment in his own car, he let his chin sag down to his breastbone. But only for a few hasty breaths. His exhaustion turned to panic as sounds of the growing firefight drew near.

Soon he'd be in the middle of the kill zone.

He wriggled from left to right, but the nylon cords held him bound to the seat. His assailant was an expert at what he did, and judging from the bloody racket that came from the stronghold, his business was killing.

But why take him? Giamante thought. He was innocent. This wasn't his fight.

The question vanished beneath a cold blanket of fear as footsteps sounded in the brush, stopping suddenly when they reached the car.

Giamante tensed, expecting the final shot.

Then he saw who it was.

The madman had come back. He was standing beside the car, looking down at Giamante like a captured creature in a cage.

"Time for the second act," Bolan said. He displayed the long blade he'd taken from Giamante's boot sheath, the polished metal gleaming in the moonlight.

"They'll see us," Giamante hissed, staring at the dagger he kept well honed and polished.

"That's the idea."

Suddenly the fear and the rage that had been building in Giamante vanished. It was replaced by a calmness he'd seldom encountered before. There was no out for him except for the out this man decided to give him, and he was tired of squirming like a trussed-up animal.

"Cut me," Giamante stated, "or cut me loose."

The Executioner met his bravado with a grim smile. "If I wanted you dead, you'd be in hell by now." He slashed down with the blade and cut through the cords. Then he threw the knife into the ground, burying the blade to the hilt.

Giamante rubbed his wrists and stretched his legs to get the circulation flowing again.

Hard voices came up the hill, calling back and forth to one another like a group of hunters flushing out game.

"Give me my gun," the Italian said. "They'll be on us anytime now."

"I figure we got about two minutes before they reach us," Bolan said. "They're hungry for blood, but I threw a bit of caution into them."

"I need my gun!"

"No can do," Bolan told him. "I left it back there." He nodded toward the stronghold. "You want it bad enough, all you've got to do is walk through the front door and pick it up."

Giamante shook his head in disbelief as the impact sank in. The gun would be traced to him. It was as much a part of his personality as the tailored suits he wore. Too many people had seen him flash it around.

He glanced over his shoulder. The voices were getting closer now. Soon the Sinistra gunners would tumble into the clearing and find the car. He doubted they would be in the mood for explanations.

"All right, let's get out of here," Giamante said. "You still got the key?"

"The car stays here," the Executioner replied. "Just in case they're too stupid to connect you and the piece." He looked back in the direction of his pursuers, gauging the progress of the kill team.

"Out of the car," the warrior demanded.

Giamante followed him into the shadows, moving far away from the sports car, which would serve like a beacon in the moonlight when the search party came this way.

"You got to give me a weapon," Giamante said.

"Sure." Bolan offered him an old Browning that he'd picked up from one of the slain Sinistra gunmen. The barrel of the weapon was scarred with scrapes and rust, probably a family heirloom passed down through generations of hardmen.

Giamante snatched the weapon like a drowning man who'd been thrown a rope. His hand curled around the grip, his finger around the trigger. Then a cold look passed across his eyes, like steel shutters cutting off the last vestiges of fear.

He was no longer caged. No longer unarmed.

The Executioner first watched the eyes as the Jekyll and Hyde transformation took place. The pleading look was gone now.

The barrel of the Browning swung halfway toward Bolan before coming to a complete stop.

"In case you're thinking of killing me," Bolan said, "you're a few rounds light." He displayed the clip of slugs for the emptied pistol.

Then the Sinistra team opened up.

Automatic bursts streaked through the darkness, scything through the trees and brush, tearing bark loose and chopping branches clean through. The leaf-laden branches rustled and shushed in an endless cascade to the ground.

A few moments later a stream of autofire plinked into the spotless sports car, causing Giamante to cry out as if he'd been wounded.

They were firing wildly, too faraway to have any accuracy. But they'd make up for it in volume soon enough.

"First one's on me," Bolan said, crouching in the darkness and propping himself against a stout tree trunk as he pressed the wire stock against his shoulder.

He listened to running footsteps scurrying through the woods, tracking the course by sound. Then he squeezed off a triple burst at the closest hitter. There was a scream, then silence.

Giamante watched the machinelike precision of the Executioner, the coolness under fire. He knew right then he would be outgunned no matter how much ordnance he brought to the table. "Whatever your reasons for bringing me into this," he said, "and whoever you are, I can help straighten things out."

"Live through this and you might be worth talking to," Bolan replied. He tossed him the clip for the Browning, then vanished into the trees.

And the war he started between Sinistra and Giamante's people raged on behind him.

5

Corbin Magnus came from a long line of royalty.

Secret royalty.

His family had been involved in Italy's military and intelligence services for generations, often reaching to the upper echelons. It showed in his carriage as he crossed the stone terrace of the restaurant on the outskirts of Milan and walked toward the white-clothed table where Mack Bolan waited.

The man was in his sixties but still looked powerful and fit, as if the sheer force of his will was keeping the years away. His face was tanned and weathered, creased by years of clandestine battles. His dark hair was combed straight back, streaked with lines of gray that made Bolan think of a wolverine, a creature always ready to jump.

Women were still drawn to him. That was obvious by their appraising stares as they followed the progress of Magnus and his retinue through the sun-splashed terrace of the restaurant.

It was either his good looks or his money that caught their eye, Bolan thought. Whichever it was, Corbin Magnus had plenty of both.

The maître d' and a handful of waiters hovered near Magnus's group. As they approached Bolan's table, most of his aides and bodyguards dropped back.

But one stayed by his side.

She was short, little more than five feet tall, and worlds apart from the type of slim-hipped models featured in Magnus's fashion magazines. Full-hipped and full-figured, she was wrapped in a soft green dress with a teardrop bodice, and Bolan wondered where she fit in with Magnus. According to his file, Magnus had one child only. And though this one was young enough to be his daughter...

"Signore Belasko," Magnus said, nodding slightly while he shook his hand. "So good of you to come." With a flourish he turned to his left and introduced the raven-haired woman. "This is Victoria Celine."

"A pleasure," Bolan said, taking her hand.

"That remains to be seen," she replied, leaning forward to speak so only Bolan could hear.

The warrior smiled. Victoria intrigued him. Not just because of her beauty. There had to be a reason why Magnus brought her to what was supposed to be a confidential sit-down. So far Bolan and the Italian covert chieftain had communicated only by proxy, through Hal Brognola. The head Fed handled all the details, right down to establishing Bolan's cover as a negotiator for an insurance company handling the Magnus situation.

At the outset, only Magnus was supposed to know who he really was. Since this was a get-acquainted meeting, Bolan had to wonder what the woman's role was.

He waited out the obligatory small talk during their meal, deflecting several more flirtations from Victoria Celine. For the most part her coquettishness was a mask, he thought. She was using her beauty to distract him while Corbin Magnus studied his responses.

And then there was the wine. That too was part of the setup, giving Magnus a chance to probe for any weakness. Bolan figured Magnus had given the waiters instructions earlier to keep the glasses filled — just to see how often Bolan had his filled.

The warrior understood the precautions. He'd seen a good number of men in the field ruined by booze, drugs or piles of bribe money that came their way, just some of the arrows that had to be dodged along with the bullets. The Executioner let the wine sit untouched throughout the meal, sticking to mineral water. Not just to please Magnus. He needed a clear head for the murky waters he would soon have to wade through.

They weren't there to compare notes on the food or pass the time of day, although that was the impression Magnus tried to give to anyone who might be looking on.

Magnus wasted no opportunity to heap praise on Victoria, whom he branded as one of the star writers for the Magnus chain of newspapers and magazines. She did a lot of behind-the-scenes work—research, special projects, investigative articles. According to Magnus she had access to all levels of society. She knew how to appeal to the common man as well as the world of haute couture.

She bowed curtly, mischievously arching her eyebrows at the praise.

"I'll have to look at your stuff sometime," Bolan said.

"All you have to do is ask."

For the rest of the meal Magnus carried on like a man without a care in the world. If Bolan hadn't known the desperate circumstances that had brought them together, he might have bought the picture.

Decades of training enabled the security man to shield his true feelings—except for one brief moment when he shook his head and spoke his daughter's name softly, almost like a sigh. "Sylvia," he said. "God help you." It was almost as if he could see her locked away somewhere, suffering.

Then he looked hard at Bolan. "Your help will also be needed, Signore Belasko. Until our own people are free to move, we will be counting on you a good deal."

"That's why I'm here. There's a lot we have to go over. But before we do so…" He directed his gaze at Victoria, who was sipping from a long-stemmed glass of Soave, her eyes dancing across the rim of the glass while she watched Bolan.

"You may speak in confidence," Magnus said. "Whatever is said at this table stays with the three of us."

"I don't think so," Bolan replied, sitting back in his chair and folding his arms in front of him.

"Please think again. Didn't our mutual friend inform you of the arrangement?"

"Yeah, he did," Bolan said, remembering Brognola explaining that Magnus would have a backup agent, someone to handle liaison and logistics and provide leads for the Executioner. "Our mutual friend told me there would be a backup man on the scene to coordinate operations."

"There's your man." Magnus nodded toward the raven-haired reporter.

"Nice disguise," Bolan commented.

"Actually," Magnus said, "it appears there may have been a misunderstanding between me and our friend. I told him there would be a backup operative we could both rely on. But you have nothing to worry about with Victoria. She is close to me."

"Too close perhaps," Bolan said. "No offense, but I need someone who can handle themselves in a crunch."

Magnus nodded sharply. "That is why she is so perfect. She *can* handle herself. Yet no one will suspect her. More than anyone else, Victoria has a reason to be around the scene. Making the rounds of her contacts. Asking questions of one and all. She is free to cover the case no matter where she goes. Whatever she does, it will seem like she's just on the job.''

"Perfect, yeah,'' Bolan said. "A perfect target.''

"You are forgetting one thing, Signore Belasko. True, your life may depend upon her. But so does mine. And so does my daughter's. I would not bring Victoria in on this if I had any doubts about her. She is a tremendous asset for all of us.''

Victoria looked unconcerned. She knew the outcome. Magnus was in her corner and that meant she was in all the way.

Bolan could see that they'd worked in tandem before. Like players on the same team, they knew each other's move before it was made. For a moment he wondered about Magnus's mental capacity. Perhaps his judgment was clouded by the situation. With his daughter abducted by an underworld clan known to murder their victims, it was a miracle he had held up this well.

"I wish I could put you at ease,'' Magnus said. "Victoria is a reporter like you are a negotiator. While both of you can handle those tasks, you can also handle a whole lot more.''

"You give me no choice,'' Bolan told him. "Other than walking away from the operation. And since our mutual friend promised my help, you can depend on it.''

"Your assistance is most welcome, Signore Belasko. I have heard nothing but the best about you.''

Bolan shrugged and said, "And I've heard good things about you." Then he glanced at Victoria. "But be prepared to lose your asset there. She'll get no special treatment from me. Nor can she expect any quarter from the people we go after."

"She knows the rules."

"Then I'll work with her."

"I assure you, Signore Belasko, that I am most capable."

"All right, then," Bolan said, knowing the issue couldn't be forced. "Let's get down to it."

Magnus nodded. Then he outlined his operations in Milan, his contacts in the Carabinieri and the forces he could muster once the Sinistra position was located. Until then he would appear to toe the line and wait for further word from the kidnappers. "I regard Sinistra's threat that they can keep tabs on the Carabinieri as legitimate. Until the issue is resolved, I need an invisible presence."

"I understand," Bolan said. He knew that no security service was totally safe from infiltration.

Though the Carabinieri was a top-flight paramilitary group, there were nearly one hundred thousand of them spread thoughout the country, working under the ministry of defence. With such great numbers there was always the chance that some of them had gone bad. Perhaps some of the members owed allegiance to one of the crime clans. Or maybe it was just a case of one of the clerks in communications unwittingly giving sensitive information to Sinistra contacts.

It was hard to tell where the leaks came from.

Until he was absolutely sure of his own people, Magnus would have to move slowly. But in the meantime he was vetting his operatives. When the time came he would have a trusted inner core to send into the fray.

Until then Bolan would be on the line, practically alone. Though Victoria looked more like a pampered movie star than a covert operator, he would give her the benefit of the doubt. If she worked out, fine. If she went down, so be it.

He couldn't afford to baby-sit anyone in the field. There was no time to coach her along.

The latest communication from Sinistra had arrived. Like the others it was a spliced-together cassette tape that instructed Magnus to begin gathering a million dollars. The same demands had been made on the Condorri family.

"Believe me," Magnus said. "I will pay the ransom in an instant. But from past experience, I know how they play this game. In some cases there is a one-time ransom. The money is dropped and the victims are freed. A very simple matter."

Magnus paused, the weight of his daughter's condition bearing down on him. Somehow he suspected it wouldn't be simple. "In other cases they bleed you to death like leeches. The kidnappers ask for a bit of money at a time. First they want an installment—just to show good faith, you understand. Then they ask for a little more—just to tide them over while they work out the details. And of course, since we're all working in this together and no one wants to upset the negotiations, that money will be paid. Then they set up another drop. A bigger one. But the money is never enough. They ask for more and more, sometimes stretching it out up to a year or more. Who knows what can happen in a year?''

The answer was in his eyes. Magnus was close to breaking down. The strain of dealing with the guilt, the fear, the need to retaliate was catching up to him.

Victoria took over when Magnus lapsed into a brooding silence. ''We estimate she and Giancarlo have a fifty-fifty chance of survival unless we recover them soon. Of all the groups we studied, Sinistra has the most mercurial leadership. Sometimes they return the victims in perfect physical condition and...'' She glanced sideways at Magnus and lowered her voice. ''And sometimes not. Kidnapping is not always the main thing with them. Ransom is not always the key. Killing is often the thing. Making a name. Spreading terror. It is hard to tell what they have in mind.''

''I've encountered that syndrome before,'' Bolan said. ''I put their chances at fifty-fifty or worse. The longer it goes, the worse the odds. She'll get further and further out of our control. Sinistra may decide to cut and run at any time.''

"Then you must act quickly," Magnus told him. "Do whatever must be done." For a moment he looked his age. No longer was he an immortal covert operative. Now he was just an aging man who could no longer control his destiny. Or his daughter's.

"I think the action has already started," Victoria said. "There was a lot of activity in the hills the other night."

"Yes," Magnus agreed, the timbre coming back into his voice. "A most interesting coincidence, Signore Belasko. All of a sudden the crime clans have gone to war with one another...exactly when you appeared on the scene." He saluted Bolan with a tilt of his glass.

"Luck is smiling on us," the warrior replied, returning the salute with a tilt of his water glass. "With the clans occupied with one another, it should be easier for us to negotiate with them."

"I think it's more than luck. I also think your cover as my negotiator will not last very long. You are taking us down a road where we can't turn off. I hope it is the right way."

"It's the only way. There's more risk involved if we just sit still and let them dictate the course."

Magnus smoothed his hands out on the table. "Understand me, Signore Belasko. I fear for my daughter. I also fear these people will find out... other things about me and my past. If they realize who they have in their possession, there will be no end to the misery they can cause us." He clenched his fist and said, "I should have prevented this—"

"No," Bolan said. "They always find a way." He glanced past Magnus at the retinue of armed bodyguards and aides sipping espresso at the other tables. Along with the ones who'd come in with Magnus, there were several other discreetly armed men whom Bolan had spotted when he first arrived at the restaurant. The covert operator's people had probably been occupying the restaurant for the past few hours.

He had solid security, Bolan thought. But not enough to cover Villa Condorri. The Condorri security team had proved to be the weak link in the chain.

"Before we go further," Bolan said, "I have to know the position of the Condorris."

"What do you mean?" Victoria asked.

"Is there a chance they were involved? It wouldn't be the first time someone arranged their own kidnapping—or someone from their family. I have to know."

"There's nothing to know!" Victoria snapped. "Giancarlo would never do something like that."

"You know him that well?"

Her face reddened. "Enough to know he and Sylvia were absolutely perfect for each other. They were in love. It was real." She sounded hurt when she spoke, almost as if she were jealous. "He wouldn't put either of them in jeopardy."

"I see." This was the first time the woman had lost her control since the meeting began. Though she quickly regained her composure, it gave him a chance to see beneath the mask for a moment. She was more than just decoration. There was a fire burning inside her. "What about the elder Condorri?"

"We checked him out long ago," Magnus said. "Back when Sylvia and Giancarlo first were attracted to each other. Condorri is financially stable. He has nothing to gain by this. Nor would he endanger his son. He is a grieving man, not a collaborator."

"I might want to check him out myself," Bolan said. "Can that be arranged?"

"Of course," Magnus replied. "Whatever you wish."

"I wish I could tell you it was going to be all right," Bolan said, pushing himself back from the table and standing up. "All I can tell you is I'll give it everything I've got to get her back."

Magnus nodded. Then his gaze shifted north suddenly, toward the Alps. The steel was back in his eyes. If will alone was enough, he'd move those mountains to get his daughter.

A good man to have behind you when the bullets started to fly, Bolan thought. Of course, that same man might throw him to the wolves if it meant the difference between getting Sylvia back or not. He'd seen it too many times before. In the end it was every man for himself, consequences and bystanders be damned. Everyone ducked when the hammer came down.

He shook hands with Magnus, then took Victoria's proffered hand.

"You and I have a lot to talk about," she said.

"You're the reporter. Get me some leads and we'll talk all you want."

On his way out, Bolan glanced at the security team sprinkled throughout the restaurant, most of them failing to look inconspicuous. And then, in the back of the restaurant, he saw a heavyset bespectacled man with neat, dark hair working at his salad. He looked harmless. And he looked slow.

It was Roland, the man from the embassy adjunct in Milan who'd been sent to look after Bolan. And though at the moment he seemed to be more interested in the wine list, Bolan knew the man was worth his weight in lead.

Roland was a one-man arsenal, the man who took care of Bolan's firepower needs.

And if things went the way he planned, Bolan thought, Roland would soon be working overtime.

6

"Wake up, Sleeping Beauty."

The woman on the floor stirred, and her mind dragged slowly from the refuge of sleep. A warm wind of dust swam across her parched skin as Faust stamped his running shoes on the floor.

Sylvia Magnus looked up, shielding her eyes from the bright afternoon sun.

He stood in the open doorway of the shed and looked down on her huddled form, enjoying the sight. Sylvia looked as weak and helpless as a kitten. No longer was she a pampered princess of Milan.

"Giancarlo?" she said weakly, still disoriented from her interrupted slumber. In that state between sleeping and waking, she was trying to bring her dreams to life. And in those dreams Giancarlo was free.

But now the real world had come knocking at her door.

"Sorry to disappoint you," Faust said. "But Giancarlo is all tied up at the moment."

"You bastard!" she cried, her dry raspy voice cracking under the effort.

"Save your breath. You'll need it."

Sylvia was still prone, moving like a newborn as she pushed her hands against the floor and craned her neck back to stretch her cramped and unused muscles.

She was deteriorating right on schedule, he thought. Time was doing his work for him, rationing out another share of despair with each passing day—just as his men were rationing out only enough food and water to keep them alive.

And there was fear working on her. He could read that in her tentative movements. What did the Sinistra crew have in mind for her? That question was always on a woman's mind when there were so many hard-looking men around. And that was one of the reasons why he chose them. He employed psychological warfare as well as physical. His prisoners had to be trained just right to carry out the role he had cast them in.

Finally there was the sense of abandonment. She had to be wondering where her father was.

Perhaps he should tell her he was printing a special edition in one of his sensation-mongering tabloids. *Extra! Extra! Read All About Kidnapped Heiress In The Hands Of Underworld Killers.* But joking around like that would make him seem too human.

"What do you want from me?" Sylvia asked. She was fully awake now, his menacing presence putting her on alert. With slow cramped muscles, she rose to a sitting position and draped his jacket over her like a shawl. Along with the swimsuit she wore at the time of her abduction, that was still the only clothing she had. By now she wasn't hesitant at all about wearing his jacket. Especially when the others looked in on her.

"Just checking my investment portfolio," Faust said, folding his arms across his chest and studying her like a butterfly mounted under glass.

She was dirty and hungry. Totally dependent upon him. His kind of girl exactly.

"You look like a million dollars," he murmured, letting his eyes linger over every inch of her figure as if he really were calculating her net worth.

When she looked back at him she was painfully aware of the contrast between them. He was dressed in a white crew neck T-shirt and black creaseless pants. His face was tan from the sun and he looked like he was on a holiday.

Sylvia had an unhealthy pallor about her. It came from being cooped up in the decrepit shed and from being cut off from the easy life she'd known. It came from the fear and uncertainty ravaging her peace of mind. It had turned her into a wreck in an incredibly short time. Aware of how she must really look to her captor, she turned away.

"Maybe even more than a million," he said, continuing to taunt her. "Of course, that still hasn't been decided yet."

"If you want to collect your million," she croaked through dry lips, "you'd better get me some water."

"That sounds like a threat. Carry it out. Go ahead. Die on us. There are plenty more where you came from. Just waiting for the taking."

"All I want is some water."

"As you wish, princess." Faust backed up a few steps and moved past the guard who waited outside. Then he dipped a long metal ladle into the bucket of water they kept for her in the shade on the side of the shed. He splashed it around loudly, torturing the thirsting woman.

When he stepped back inside, she leaned forward on her knees and reached out her hands for the ladle.

He flung the water in her face.

It drenched her skin, the rivulets tracking moist paths down her face and shoulders, then onto the floor.

With an animallike scream, Sylvia used her last bit of strength to push up off the floor and propel herself toward her tormentor with outstretched arms. Her fingernails slashed at his face in a raking motion.

But she missed her target.

With the flourish of a matador, Faust stepped to the side and clacked her wrists together with the heel of his palm. She cried out in pain from the jarring impact. Then he closed his hand around her narrow wrists and tugged her forward.

The off-balance prisoner flew out the door of the shed, coming down hard on her knees on the splintery porch. Her momentum carried her forward and sent her sprawling face-first onto the ground.

Sylvia slowly rolled onto her back, gulping in air and tasting freedom for a moment. And then she tasted fear. The brief look around showed that there were more than a dozen men positioned around the house. They were quiet. They were armed. They looked like men steeling themselves for war.

Faust jumped off the porch and landed with a thump beside her, preventing her from moving any farther.

The guard who'd been silently standing by the shed hurried to her other side. He looked at his leader for directions.

Faust nodded toward the shed.

The burly guard reached down, grabbed her by the wrists and yanked her to her feet.

"Back into your cage, tiger."

Sylvia glared at Faust as the guard ushered her back to the door of her stifling prison.

The dagger-filled look reminded him of a harpy of old, an ancient hag of legend using the evil eye to curse him.

His hand lashed out at her face. It was a precise and loud slap, leaving a blossoming imprint on her cheek.

"Don't forget who owns you now," he said, "and don't push your luck with me. If thine eyes offend me, I'll pluck them out."

While the guard threw her inside and locked the door behind her, Faust walked over to the shed on the far side of the house. The hut where Giancarlo was kept. It was like stereo, he thought, both of them kept nicely in matching hovels.

He opened the door quickly, letting the brutal sun shine down on the prisoner.

Giancarlo looked up at him through bruised eyes. His cheeks were swollen from fresh punishment.

This one never knew when to stop, Faust thought.

Even now Giancarlo pulled at the ropes that bound him to a cross beam on the wall. No matter how many times he was beaten, the younger Condorri kept trying to fight them. He swore and cursed and tugged at the ropes, stopping short of foaming at the mouth while he stared up at his captor.

"You're a stubborn man. And brave. An admirable quality."

"I'll...get...back at you...."

"Admirable," Faust repeated, "but suicidal. You must learn when to stop fighting us." He nodded at the guard who'd followed him into the shed. "Otherwise, we'll have to keep on teaching you."

The guard kicked Giancarlo in the stomach. The carefully aimed blow would have doubled him over if the rough ropes cutting into his skin allowed him any movement.

"Do you understand what I'm talking about, Giancarlo?" Faust said. "No? Then we'll leave you with something to think about."

Like lightning striking again, the guard kicked him in the same spot.

Giancarlo fell silent, his head slumping back against the wall.

"Much better. Now if you'll excuse me, I have business to attend to."

TWO HOURS LATER Amory Faust arrived at his Lake Maggiore villa, driving his Mercedes at the head of a caravan of jeeps, sports cars and station wagons.

Just like the businessmen he preyed upon, Faust needed a place to unwind, a retreat where he could get away from the pressures of his trade.

This retreat was also a fortress. The main house was carved out of the side of a hill, flanked by a number of smaller buildings for guests. Since the villa was leased in the name of a fictitious corporation, it wasn't unusual for a large group to descend upon it.

It was common practice for many a Milano executive to bring his staff out for a lakeside session at a private retreat. A working vacation in the crisp country air.

Though Faust's "executives" passed inspection from a distance, a closer look at the men climbing the white stone steps cut into the hill might have shown that half of them weren't accustomed to wearing suits or behaving like landed gentry. The Sinistra hardman couldn't just waltz in there with an army of shotgun-toting bruisers. Until it was time to go into action they would have to maintain their cover as gentlemen.

The disguise came much easier to Faust, who'd lived among the upper class for years at a stretch, learning their ways and their weaknesses. He'd done it much the same way a man behind enemy lines would, mimicking their behavior until they took him as one of their own. It gave him a safe identity to hide behind until those times when he needed to replenish the coffers.

Now was such a time.

His guests were gunmen. They were Sinistra's very own insurance agency. If he wanted to stay in the business, he had to hit back hard. And he had to do it fast. Amory Faust had to be a name that still inspired fear in friend and enemy alike.

He and Donato led the way into the main house, followed by his board of directors who quickly set down briefcases that were all much heavier than they looked, loaded with enough weaponry to wage a small war.

That was exactly why Faust had summoned them to the villa. He could have held the war council at a number of other Sinistra safehouses, but this place was his own.

Plus there was another overwhelming advantage.

Lake Maggiore was situated on the Italian-Swiss border. If things got out of hand, a short trip north would take him to Switzerland where he'd already established another respectable alias, complete with a number of Swiss accounts.

But Amory Faust didn't intend to let things get out of hand. If war came calling, he would answer in kind.

He wasted little time in getting the council started, detailing a couple of the men to distribute pitchers of water, wine and ashtrays.

Like executives planning their assaults on the marketplace, nearly a dozen members of Sinistra sat around a long oval table on the top floor of the main house.

Wall-length windows and sliding glass doors provided a stunning view of Lake Maggiore, a dark shimmering mirror swimming with reflected lights from shore. The windows also provided a view of all the approaches to the villa.

Soon smoke filled the room as the council got down to business.

"We all know the reason why we're here," Faust said, looking from face to face. "It is because of that reason that some of us are no longer here." Like a priest, he spoke of the recently departed brethren— their good deeds, their service in the Sinistra cause.

Then he stared at Lacazino, the ox-shouldered gunman sitting at the opposite end of the table. His seat at the table had been no accident. There he faced the cold eyes of Amory Faust, who had put more men in their graves than were gathered in the room.

Lacazino sat there stoically, wrapped in an ill-fitting suit and the knowledge that he might not walk away from the table.

"Say what you have to say," Faust demanded.

Lacazino looked around the faces of the table. Most of the men he knew. They'd moved up through the ranks of the Sinistra clan over the years, hard-faced survivors who'd do whatever it took to make a living, which often meant making a killing.

For a moment he locked eyes with Donato, who was Faust's right-hand man now. But there had been a time when Lacazino and Donato were close. They used to run in the same pack when they were both young Turks. But that didn't count for much now.

Donato would kill him in a minute if he had to.

Any man at the table would.

Of course, Lacazino wouldn't go down without a struggle. He had his own rules to live by. And to die by. He sat there with his hands folded like a penitent, but they were also close to his holstered automatic beneath his jacket. If he saw a bullet coming his way, he'd take down his killer.

Then they'd have an eternity together to sort out the right or wrong of it.

"I got nothing much to say," Lacazino said. "Except we were hit out of the blue. Hell, out the black! No one saw this guy until he was right on top of us. Whoever he was, he was a pro. One of the best I've seen."

Some of the men at the table laughed, especially the younger ones who mocked his excuse. They'd made their kills, but rarely against someone who fired back.

Lacazino craned his bull neck forward and shifted his body slightly, the motion silencing the scoffers. He was in his fifties, and if anything, had grown even more powerful over the years. "He could have taken out anyone at this table," he said, his raspy voice a soft threat.

"You got away quick enough," Faust observed.

"Yeah, I did. Bullets were flying everywhere, but he just stood there, dishing it out. I got off a few rounds but had to bail out."

Faust nodded. "You left them there."

"There was nobody home anymore. They were dead already. I would have been hit too, if I stayed. This way I could regroup the men and go after them."

"Maybe that *was* a wise move," Faust said. "That's one of the things we're here to decide. We're also here to decide how it happened."

"I told you," Lacazino said. "They took us by surprise."

"The surprise is that you didn't post enough security. You were more interested in drinking. In playing cards. Because of that, you gave the others a dead-man's hand."

"We had a man on watch."

"One man," Faust scoffed. "Just one man." He leaned forward, his feral eyes sparkling, a hawk coming in for the kill. "You were *all* supposed to be on alert!"

The heavyset soldier shrugged and sat back in the chair. Better to weather the storm than to bring more heat down on his head.

"You have one chance to redeem yourself," Faust went on. "Get this man, whoever he is, and you win back your life."

"If someone else gets him first?"

"I wouldn't let that happen if I were you."

Lacazino nodded. A reprieve of sorts had been granted. But from here on in, whichever way he turned he would find a sword hanging over his neck.

The man who'd wrecked their stronghold that night wouldn't be an easy target. Nor was Amory Faust the forgiving sort. While Lacazino had lost his friends, Faust had lost face. Since the man was in command, that was the more important of the two.

"Now we move on to other matters." Faust reached down for a small travel bag beside his chair. "Perhaps a simpler matter, perhaps not." He dropped the bag onto the table with a heavy thud, then took out the gleaming Swiss pistol that belonged to Felix Giamante. "By now you should all know who this belongs to," he said, spinning the automatic around on the table. "Felix Giamante. He is a playboy. At times he is a fool. But nonetheless he is a dangerous man. We knew that long before he moved against us."

The men around the table nodded. The Sinistra soldiers kept tabs on the other crime clans as a matter of course. The secret knowledge of crimes and criminals and their specialties that were locked inside their heads was a regular *Who's Who* of L'Anonima Sequestri. Knowing details like what strongman worked for which clan, and who was powerful and who could be stepped on, helped them stay alive.

"In case there was any doubt that this was indeed his gun," Faust said, "Felix Giamante's car was left behind at the scene."

This time there were murmurs around the table, a worried and mumbled discussion.

"Is something wrong?" Faust asked, realizing the men had obviously talked things over among themselves.

After a brief silence the Sinistra soldiers looked from face to face before finally settling on Alessandro Verga who sat in the middle of the table. "Perhaps there *is* something you've overlooked," Verga suggested.

Faust wasn't surprised that the task fell to Verga, a slender man in his forties with the mocking eyes of a man who lived on confrontation. Verga had handled a lot of Sinistra's work before Amory Faust came on the scene.

"Perhaps you are right, Sandro," Faust said. "After all, no one is infallible." He smiled broadly as he spoke. It had been a rather large mistake that took Verga down a notch in the Sinistra organization. The wrong people had been snatched on his last operation. By the time Sinistra realized their hostages could never afford to pay any ransom, the Carabinieri had closed in on the kidnap team. Four Sinistra men were killed in the shootout, along with one of the hostages.

A lot of heat came down on the organization after that fiasco. And when Sinistra finally felt ready to move again, they selected Amory Faust as their key man. Faust's first Sinistra operation earned them a lot of money and respect. So did the ones that followed.

Verga took his demotion without complaint. This was the only life he knew, and he wasn't about to abandon it even if it meant taking a back seat. He had slowly climbed back up the ladder of the organization by demonstrating total obedience and loyalty to the cause.

And maybe now he was getting ready to reclaim his position, Faust mused.

"If you have anything to say that will prevent us from, eh, committing a tragic error, go right ahead."

"I will," Verga said. "Maybe it's not much, but this has all the signs of a setup. You claim it's a war. But Felix Giamante had no need to attack us."

"No apparent need," Faust contradicted.

"His people were doing well," Verga continued. "They knew how to act in this game, how to hold their own. For Giamante to suddenly go mad and attack a crew of ours... Well, it makes no sense. Where's the profit? What does he get for taking such a risk? Except the promise of bullets."

"Yes," Faust said. "From his own gun. I plan to return it to him personally."

That earned a lot of praise from the men at the table. The subtler aspects of warfare often escaped them, but they knew the code of vengeance well. A man couldn't walk away from trouble. Otherwise he was no longer a man.

"His own gun," Verga repeated, saying it louder this time. And slower. He gave the crew plenty of time to let his words sink in, then, like a lawyer making his case, he leaned forward and said, "So he leaves his gun at the scene. A gun many people know belongs to him. We all know Giamante is a playboy. A show-off. He likes to be seen with fast cars, fast women ... and fast weapons. But for him to leave such a well-known weapon at the scene, well, an intelligent man must think twice about this."

"I have," Faust interjected.

"And an intelligent man would have to think twice about an enemy who leaves his car behind. Wouldn't a man like Giamante have the foresight to come in masked? Why would he sign his name in Sinistra blood?''

"Good questions," Faust said. "Questions I have asked myself many times. There are no easy answers. But there are facts. Giamante was seen there, fighting alongside the professional he'd hired. Or maybe the professional hired him? It doesn't matter. The fact is that Giamante was there. And he did come after us. Maybe he left his signature behind because he wants it to be known that he can walk all over us, that he is the only power that must be taken seriously. And that leaves us little choice, my friends. There is only one way to show that the Sinistra clan must be taken seriously. And that means going to war."

"War is no good for anyone," Verga stated.

Faust shook his head. "It's no good for the losers. But the winners take all. And that will be us."

The talk continued awhile longer, but most of the men had already come around to Amory Faust's way of thinking. The kidnapping business had its occupational hazards. Life in the crime clans was never untroubled. War was a part of it. Death was a part of it. And wealth beyond their wildest dreams was also a part of it.

Before the night ended, Faust had every man convinced their dreams would come true.

Almost every man.

Alesandro Verga remained unconvinced to the end. "I will go along, but I want it to be known that I am against this. I think someone is setting us up to take a fall. And I think that someone is either Magnus or Condorri. One of our pigeons is trying to throw us off the track."

"I have people looking into that," Faust told him. "The Carabinieri is standing still on this one. None of its teams are moving against us, nor are the families. I have people watching both Magnus and Condorri. So far they are cooperating fully, waiting upon my every word."

"Then maybe we should speed it up," Verga suggested. "Give them the word now. Make the switch, get the money, then take care of this other business."

"You would let others force our hand? You would subject my name to ridicule?"

"No," Verga replied, exhaling loudly and shaking his head. In resignation he pushed himself back from the table. "I have nothing more to say. Just tell me what to do and I'll do it."

Faust reached across the table and gripped his shoulder. "That is what I've been waiting to hear, Sandro. With you by my side, there is nothing to worry about."

The older man nodded. "Except for the man in black. The man that no one was able to see until he slaughtered them like wild beasts."

"His time will come," Faust said. "Whoever he is, his time will come. But first, let's see to the Giamantes."

"WHAT ABOUT THIS ONE?" Lucia suggested, holding the red dress in front of her, smoothing it out with her long manicured hands. She had platinum hair, a lithe figure, and the kind of wicked look in her eyes that kept her in furs in winter and the latest styles in summer.

At the moment she stood near the shop window of the boutique on Via Monte Napoleone, one of Milan's cobblestoned streets of haute couture.

"Well? I said, *well?* Giuseppe, look at me!"

Giuseppe Giamante sipped his cup of black coffee, puffed on his filtered cigarette, then turned his leonine head toward the former star dancer he'd plucked from one of the clan's nightclubs on Via Senato.

"I *was* looking at you," he protested.

"No!" she said, snapping her metallic mane of hair to the right. "You were looking at *her*." Her voice was filled with ice as she pointed at the salesgirl, the one with the musical laugh and a body that danced along with it, the one who always dropped whatever she was doing the moment Lucia and Giuseppe stepped into the fashionable boutique.

Giamante shrugged. "Yes. But only in self-defense. If I looked at you any longer my heart would melt."

The platinum blonde wagged her finger at him.

"Ah, what chance do I have?" the salesgirl asked. "She is willing to fight for you."

He laughed. "That one is willing to fight *me*. It's true. Believe me. You'd better be careful with Lucia. She's much stronger than she looks."

The salesgirl danced over to Lucia, telling her how lucky she was to have such a man and how wonderful her taste was in picking out the red dress.

Giamante watched it all like it was a theater. That was the main attraction of shopping here with Lucia. The boutique put on quite a show whenever they came in. The salesgirl would flirt with him and tease her, then goad her into trying on outrageously overpriced fashions. It was always the same dance. A carefully orchestrated minuet that continued until the sale was made and they would leave, sated with costly culture until the next time Lucia needed another dress and he needed some more attention.

A few moments later, Lucia had slipped into the red dress. It was long and clinging, and revealed her curves. Of course, everything Lucia wore revealed her curves. She would look good in a paper sack, he thought.

"Now tell me what you think, Giuseppe. And be honest about how stunning I look." She spun, the motion snapping the bottom of the dress like a wispy satin cloud as she whirled past a quartet of mannequins.

Giamante put out his cigarette, exhaling the smoke before walking over to study her.

"Well? What do you think?"

"I think you are even more beautiful than they are," he said, gesturing at the well-dressed mannequins.

"Giuseppe!"

"And twice as smart—"

She started to swear at him, started to laugh, then she started to scream.

Giamante was too late in deciphering what was happening. From the corner of his eye he spotted unusual motion on the street outside the shop. Something was breaking up the pattern of the pedestrians who'd been walking past the storefront window in stately procession. Some of them were moving quickly, getting out of the way of a madman on a motorcycle. Others were standing still, watching in horror as the vehicle knifed toward them.

The roar of the bike drowned out the light jazz music in the shop, the chatter of the salesgirls and the panicked screams of the window-shoppers diving out of the way.

The bike headed straight for the window, carrying two helmeted men astride the long black leather seat. The driver jumped the bike over the curb, skidding to a sideways stop that gave his passenger a broadside shot at Giamante.

It happened too fast to do anything. One moment he was drinking in Lucia's beauty, the next he was under fire. Despite the blitzkrieg attack, Giamante felt like it was all happening in slow motion.

Another bike roared down the street from the left side. A third one joined the fray from the right, zeroing in on the shop with split-second precision. Like nightmares springing into life, they seemed to appear from nowhere.

One of the bikers carried a Franchi SPAS automatic shotgun, its loud 12-bore blasts punching holes in three of Giamante's soldiers who'd been waiting outside. One moment they were walking back and forth in front of the shop, talking and smoking. The next they were bleeding and dying, ripped apart by the heavy scattergun.

Automatic fire chewed into the glass storefront, sending a stream of metal hornets whizzing inside the shop.

As the windows burst and flew into dagger-sharp shreds, the mannequins closest to the front of the store toppled, their hollowed bodies shattered by the stream of 9 mm Parabellum rounds.

Like firemen putting out a blaze, the assassins faced front and hosed the interior of the shop, squeezing off burst after burst from Beretta Model 12 submachine guns.

While glass, draperies and mannequins disintegrated all around him, Giuseppe Giamante darted toward the window, his heavy revolver feeling as clumsy as a cannon as he tried to aim it at the bikers.

He fired one shot before a bullet scorched a trough in his palm, knocking the gun free.

Then he saw the barrel of the automatic shotgun coming toward him and Lucia. The shotgunner was holding the pistol grip of the assault weapon with one hand while he took aim.

The heavy-hitting Special Purpose Assault Shotgun could fire four rounds a second and that's what it was doing, kicking hell out of the walls behind them, getting closer and closer.

He tried to grab Lucia—but then there was nothing to grab.

Her arm exploded.

The shotgun load blew off most of her arm from the elbow down. Lucia spun from the impact of the blast, screaming one more time before the next load bulldozed through her chest and put her down like a lead weight.

While her blood cascaded around him, Giuseppe dived for the dropped revolver, snatching at it with his good left hand. His right hand was slick with crimson.

A burst of 9 mm slugs singed the air over his head. Another round of shotgun blasts hammered the floor and display cases around him. And then a lightweight body fell on top of him. It was the salesgirl and she was much lighter than usual, practically headless from the full frontal blasts.

All this beauty falling around him, dying, shredding, ripped to pieces by savages. All because he couldn't take care of them. Just like his men couldn't take care of him. He'd heard only one or two shots from his own men, coming from a fourth Giamante bodyguard who was returning from the next street over. But an automatic burst silenced even that paltry counterattack.

And then the thunder stopped.

The lightning strike was over and the bikers were roaring away, leaving a slaughterhouse behind them.

Giamante knew he was their target. If they couldn't get Felix Giamante, they would go for Giuseppe. He'd known that. He'd expected it. Felix had filled him in on the bizarre attack on the Sinistra stronghold. Since then, Giuseppe Giamante had taken precautions and traveled with more protection than usual.

But that only meant more targets for Sinistra. If they couldn't hit him, they'd hit anybody who had the misfortune to be around him.

It was like a jinx, a deadly cloud hanging over his head.

The Giamante clan was cursed.

Giuseppe smacked his good hand on the floor. There were rules that were supposed to be followed by men of honor. No civilians were to be hurt. No neutral territory should be violated, especially here in the heart of Milan.

But now, as Giuseppe Giamante slid out from under the shattered remains of the salesgirl, he knew there were no more rules.

From now on nothing would be safe.

From now on he would only live for war. And he would die for it, too, if he had to.

AT THE SAME TIME as the windows blew out on Via Monte Napoleone, the club run by the Giamante clan on Via Senato was doing more business than usual for that time of the afternoon.

There were the usual number of tourist walk-ins who'd drifted into the bar along with the regulars, and a group of businessmen had also converged on the place. They'd pushed together two long tables at the back of the club near the jukebox-shaped CD player. One of the men from the table had kept the music thumping while they talked, feeding several coins into the slot.

The businessmen seemed to be waiting for something, ordering several drinks, now and then looking at their watches.

Suddenly the time was right, and two men walked behind the bar. The bartender, a solidly built middle-aged man whose hair was turning white, keyed the register open, then stood aside while one of the men removed stacks of bundled cash.

It was the usual procedure. Like clockwork the afternoon's receipts were skimmed by two Giamante soldiers.

The businessmen at the table suddenly stood. The one who'd been feeding coins into the jukebox made another selection, then turned around with a dull black Bernadelli automatic in his hand and fired two shots.

The soldiers went down.

The bartender reached for a weapon from below the counter—and flew back against the bottle-filled glass shelves with a red ditch blossoming on his forehead, shot point-blank by a Sinistra "businessman" who'd leaned over the bar and fired.

Two more shots hit the bartender before he reached the floor. His outstretched hands reached behind him for support, tumbling several liquor bottles onto the floor.

One of the Giamante enforcers burst out of the back room and into a wall of lead. The Sinistra gunmen had been waiting for him to make his move. The man was hit with such force that his hands flapped out against the door, as if nailed there by the lead slugs.

A bloody red outline remained on the door when the Giamante gunner dropped to the floor.

By now the rest of the people in the club were screaming for help, diving under tables and running for the front door. The Sinistra crew calmly stood its ground and shot up the mirrors, tables and portraits of Giamante clansmen and confederates hanging on the walls.

Then they calmly trooped out the side door like a small victorious army.

AMORY FAUST STEPPED OUT from between the parked cars in the factory-rich suburb of Milan and hurried to the driver's side of a dark green four-door sedan stuck in a traffic jam—a bottleneck artfully caused by a quartet of Sinistra drivers a half block ahead.

The driver looked at Faust just as the Sinistra henchman pointed a Swiss P-210-2 pistol at his head and pulled the trigger. Shards of window glass danced across the man's bullet-shattered forehead, the loud shots cutting off his unintelligible protests.

The car lurched forward and crashed into the tail end of the car in front of it, locking bumpers in a hopeless entanglement of chrome and rubber.

Faust had kept pace with the car, training the P-210-2 on the man in the passenger seat. He squeezed the trigger carefully, blasting the man's temple away while he scrambled for his own weapon lost beneath his jacket, lost because of his slow-moving, fear-charged reflexes.

Then Faust turned toward the two other passengers who sat in the back seat.

One of them was already dead, his white shirt a blotchy flag of blood from the 9 mm rounds Donato had pumped into him from his position on the other side of the car. The Giamante enforcer had been looking at Faust when Donato fatally surprised him.

That left one survivor.

The last passenger was a brown-haired woman who was trying to fly. She leaped across the dead man and clawed at the door, finally tumbling out onto the street—and found herself looking up into the barrel of Donato's automatic.

The gunner glanced at Faust for direction.

With a nod of his head, the Sinistra captain called off the hit. While Donato backed away, Faust helped the woman to her feet.

She was shaking uncontrollably as he gripped her elbow and ushered her to the sidewalk. "Understand me," he said softly.

The woman shook her head, unable to talk.

"I said, *understand me!*"

"Yes, yes, I do. I will. I—"

"Shut up," Faust hissed.

She clamped her teeth together, eager to obey.

Faust glanced back at the open door of the sedan where her riding partner was crumpled down in the seat with his mammoth head twisted at an awkward angle over his breastbone.

"Take a good look at that," he ordered.

The woman forced herself to turn back to the scene of the slaughter that she'd so narrowly escaped.

"Tell Felix Giamante that we will first cut off the feet of his organization. Then the arms. And finally the head of the clan himself. Unless Giamante comes out of hiding it will be a long and brutal war. War to the end. He will be the last of his Family to live. But only for a short while. Can you tell him that?''

The woman nodded.

''Then we are finished,'' Faust said. He smiled and sent her on her way. ''Make sure you give him my regards,'' he said, waving the silvery Swiss pistol in the air.

7

Streaks of gray clouds moved across the jagged sky-line of Monte Cappelli, its lights etching a hazy electric halo against the palette of night.

On most nights the distant silhouette of the village was a beautiful and soothing sight. But the men who watched in the dead of night weren't concerned about the glorious view.

The Giamante hardmen were waiting for an army to descend upon the safehouse in the foothills of Monte Cappelli, one of Felix Giamante's love nests that had been turned into a machine-gun nest.

A half dozen of the Giamante clansmen had come to the whitewashed stone cottage set back from one of the narrow country roads that spiderwebbed down the lush green hills from Monte Cappelli.

It looked like a fairy-tale cottage to anyone who gave it a second look. It was immaculately kept, with a waist-high stone wall shielding the landscaped lawn from the road. A latticework gazebo with wicker chairs and tables occupied the left side of the cottage grounds, and on the right was a neatly kept garden.

Everyone was going to ground. The Giamantes. The Sinistra clansmen. Felix had five men with him. His brother Giuseppe was recovering from his wounds in a seaside villa on the Portofina Peninsula that the Family normally used for a holiday retreat. Now the villa on the Eastern Riviera coastline was just a retreat.

Other members of the Giamante Family were spread out in countryside enclaves and apartment houses from Milan to Pavia and all the way down to the Riviera. They were all within fighting distance, most of them less than an hour or two away by car.

Some were hiding out. Some were looking for targets.

From the first day he'd come to the cottage, Felix Giamante tried to convince himself that he was merely regrouping until he could stop the war or launch a counterattack. But a part of his mind kept telling him he was ducking and running. It didn't really matter what he chose to call it. The important thing was that he was alive.

The five men garrisoned with him shared a twenty-four-hour watch, staying inside most of the day and scanning the countryside for any sign of a Sinistra hit team.

Every night two of the men patrolled the grounds for infiltrators.

But they were looking for the wrong signs. They were expecting an attack en masse.

They weren't expecting a man who moved as quietly as an unseen breeze coiling around their necks.

MACK BOLAN CROUCHED at the edge of the stone wall, shadows of leaves from the trees above him falling over his dark form. He wore a balaclava hood pulled over his head, and a black combat vest that matched the rest of his night-shift garb.

His Beretta 93-R was sheathed in leather under his left arm, and he carried additional ordnance in the pockets of his combat vest. But the main weapon he was using this night was a long rifle with a dull black barrel.

The Executioner rested the rifle barrel in a crevice in the wall that he'd spotted during his earlier recon.

And then he waited.

Footsteps sounded to his left. They were stealthy, but to a trained ear it was a dead giveaway.

Accent on dead.

The guard came out into the open, a lean shadow with a subgun slung over his shoulder and his arm at rest on top of the barrel. He was looking straight ahead along the perimeter just like he'd been doing all night.

It was almost a crime, Bolan thought, as he took aim, exhaling softly as he squeezed the trigger.

There was a soft snapping sound, little more than a pop.

The man came to a complete stop as the slug drilled into his neck. His knees bent, his vocal cords froze, and his mind tumbled down a black hole. His body followed, dropping to the ground, totally unconscious now that the navigator had bailed out.

Bolan held his fire. He'd been ready to trigger a second shot until he saw the way the man went down.

He climbed over the wall and approached the fallen guard, training the barrel of the needle rifle on him by reflex. The shell of the needle-headed soluble bullet had penetrated the skin, then disintegrated while the narcotic load flooded the man's bloodstream.

The men who had developed the chemical concoction called it an "ice pick" because of the way it seemed to flash-freeze anyone who got hit. Bolan didn't know the full makeup of the loads, just that the mad-scientist's rifle knocked the target down like a steamroller, flattening him out with a phenocyclethylamine and sodium pentathol kick.

There were nine more needle-nosed loads in the stick clip and a spare clip in the side pocket of his combat vest. He could have come in lethal tonight, but killing a man's bodyguards wasn't the best way to win his trust.

Bolan pressed the tip of his foot into the sentry's side and pushed hard, testing the man's reaction. There was none.

The black-clad Executioner took the guard's place, matching the man's slow and deliberate pace as he neared the rendezvous point with the second guard forty yards away.

The warrior picked out the other man's shape first and held the barrel of the needle gun steady as he continued to advance.

The second guard called out softly at Bolan's approach. It was the standard pattern they'd been following all night. One man called, the other man answered, then they passed each other to make another round.

Sometimes they'd talked to each other for a minute or two to pass the time.

It was an easy pattern to fall into.

And an easy pattern to get knocked out of.

Bolan closed the gap between them by the time the man called out again, answering him with a pull of the trigger.

The man cried out and slapped at his neck but didn't reach it in time. Then his hand waved in midair, suspended in slow motion as the fingers reached out toward Bolan almost as if he were trying to warn him.

The Executioner fired again just to make sure.

By the time the second needle bullet hit him, the guard was already teetering on weakened knees. His body spun, weighted by the mind-blanking ice-pick load. Then he landed with a soft thud on the grass.

Bolan tested this one, too. After several probes of his foot he was convinced the man was out. The knockout shots worked as well as Roland had promised.

Roland's intel at this point was also right on target, Bolan thought as he scanned the rest of the perimeter with a handheld nightvision scope. There were no man-size creatures prowling around the walls.

Two of the hardmen were down for the count, which left, according to Roland, four more in the house.

The warrior dropped to the ground and slowly worked his way along the shadowed terrain, stopping now and then to study the cottage. The place was mapped out in his head, right down to the blueprints. He knew every inch of ground he had to cover.

Roland had used his pull to drop an invisible net over the operations of the Giamante clan. The Italian police and organized crime units had collected a massive amount of data on the Giamante brothers, data that Roland had informally gleaned without giving away how interested the consulate was. He had friends throughout the services, friends who didn't mind releasing some sensitive information to their clandestine brethren if it could do some good.

It had.

The combined intel reeled in by Roland and other consulate spies provided a guided tour through the Giamante underworld—the bank accounts, the silent partnerships with semilegitimate businesses in

Milan and several other cities in the north. And all of the real-estate holdings the clan possessed had been quietly bought up.

The hard intel had been gathered for years, waiting to be used on the day the Italian authorities had absolute proof of Giamante's criminal dealings.

Bolan was simply moving up the schedule a bit.

He and Roland had checked out most of the Giamante hideouts before narrowing down Felix's whereabouts to an apartment building in Milan or this snug and safe little cottage.

The Executioner had checked out the apartment building in a winding side street across from an open market where vendors and customers filled the street. The building was occupied with Giamante gunmen, but there'd been no sign of the Giamante brothers.

Roland had scoped out the country hideaway, determining the number of men, the layout of the cottage, and the most important fact of all—Felix Giamante was in residence.

Now it was time for the Executioner to renew his acquaintance with Giamante. He headed for the rear of the cottage.

Giamante had confidence in his guards, and kept some of the windows open to allow in the country breeze.

Shortly past three o'clock in the morning, more than a breeze slipped through the screen of the vacant room at the back of the cottage. There was no one around to detect the intrusion. The two guards who usually bunked there were now sleeping on the ground alongside the perimeter wall, thanks to the ice-pick nightcaps.

Bolan clipped through the screen, pushing it aside like paper as he stepped softly onto the floor. He paused for a moment to see if there was any other sound. Nothing. The house was his.

He made his way down the hall. The remaining two relief guards were sleeping in a room off to the left of the hall, waiting for their shift. And in the darkened front room was the last on-duty guard. He was almost awake, sitting in a chair by the window in a state of half sleep. A submachine gun rested across his legs.

The Executioner stepped quickly across the carpeted floor, the barrel of the needle gun rising like a magnet drawn toward the back of the man's neck. The guard stirred, then settled back into his near comatose state.

When he was close enough to be sure of his target, Bolan pulled the trigger.

The needle stung the back of the hardman's neck, causing him to raise his head for a moment. Then his chin sank sharply onto his chest.

Bolan stepped around to the front of the chair to check him out. The guard was down and out.

The Executioner took care of the two sleeping sentries, then headed toward a stairway that led up to the master bedroom.

The nest of Felix Giamante.

Bolan made it to the top of the stairs before he heard movement inside the room.

He leaped forward, kicked the door open and charged into the room just as Giamante was swinging his legs over the side of the bed and reaching for a holstered automatic slung around the bedpost.

"Don't try it!" Bolan growled.

But Giamante was desperate, thinking that somehow the Sinistra gunmen had tumbled onto him. He wasn't going to wait for a bullet to finish him off, not without trying to put up a fight.

Bolan rushed the Italian, shoving him face-first into the bed board before he could unholster his automatic.

But Giamante still had a lot of fight left in him. His right elbow slashed back for Bolan's head, fanning past his temple in a blurring motion.

It would have been a killing blow if the warrior hadn't anticipated the strike. He ducked and shoved the rifle barrel forward like a pitchfork, gouging it into the back of Giamante's neck until the cold metal rifle barrel held him spellbound.

"It's your choice," Bolan said. "I didn't come here to kill you. I came to talk."

"You!" Giamante recognized the voice. He turned, caught his breath, then looked up at the hooded Executioner as he stepped back with the barrel.

"Yeah. It's me. Again. Wherever you are, I can find you."

"What do you want?"

"Cooperation."

"You got a funny way of asking." Giamante rubbed the back of his neck where the barrel had bit into him. Then, as if it just occurred to him that he was supposed to be in a well-guarded safe house, Giamante said, "What about my people? What did you do with them?"

"Nothing permanent." Bolan waved the rifle barrel toward his captive. "This only knocked them out for a while."

"Every one of them?"

"All present and accounted for."

Giamante nodded, then studied the rifle. "And that's just a tranquilizer gun?"

"Heavier than that. These doses don't come off the shelf. When your people come around they'll feel like someone's banging a sledgehammer on their head for a day or two. But it's better than being dead."

"That's what you're offering me? You won't kill me and mine if we play along?"

"That's the gist of it," Bolan replied. "There's a few more details to work out."

"Not much of a deal."

"Better than most. Call it what you want. A deal, a truce, a free pass. Until this is over, you and I are fighting on the same side. Later on we go our own ways. We're not friends. Consider us allies."

"Allies have equal say," Giamante said.

"We both want Faust dead. That's equal enough."

"What do you expect me to do?"

"Help me find him."

"I don't work miracles. If I did, *you'd* be sleeping. Permanently."

"I don't want miracles. But I know you've got teams looking for Faust. Just like he's got teams looking for you. I figure it's only a matter of time before one of you finds the other. The way I see it, guy, it's better to do the finding than to be found. Like tonight. You were easy to find, Felix. Too easy. I could have let those sleeping soldiers lie...or die."

"If it's so easy, go find Faust yourself."

"Sinistra isn't quite as well-known as your people are," Bolan said. "Takes longer to find the headmen. But believe me, we're looking."

"We?"

"Some interested people."

"Who are these people?"

"You don't want to meet them."

"I'll take your word for it," Giamante replied. "If they're anything like you, I don't need any more friends."

"Allies," Bolan corrected.

"Allies. And equals." By now his drumming heartbeat was returning to normal. So was his realization that any deal worked two ways. "You want this to work out, put down the gun. I talk better when my partner isn't about to shoot me."

"Deal." Bolan lowered the rifle, but he stepped back so Giamante wouldn't be tempted to make a grab for it.

Giamante stood and threw on a black robe over his drawstring sweatpants. "Now let's go downstairs," he said, "so you can tell me why I should help the man who sent my people into war."

"After you," Bolan said, letting Giamante pass. Then he followed him down the stairs. After a quick survey of his men to make sure they were still breathing, Giamante headed for the kitchen.

They sat at a bare wooden table, talking at length, captive conspirators who needed each other to end a war that one of them had started.

Bolan carefully filed away the names and suspected locations that Giamante revealed to him so he could check them out later with Roland.

The two men set up procedures for passing information and coordinating their attacks on the Sinistra organization.

By the time they were through talking, each man was ready to try out the uneasy alliance. The alternative was to have one more enemy to watch out for.

When Bolan headed for the door, Giamante walked slowly after him and said, "Next time you visit, try knocking."

8

The Executioner walked across the spired rooftop of the Cathedral of Milan, watched closely by stone-faced angels. The white marble facade of the Gothic cathedral looked down on the city's main square, Piazza del Duomo. It was full of pigeons, parishioners and tourists who flocked to the Duomo all hours of the day to make their pilgrimage.

They'd come to pray.

He'd come to prey.

Victoria Celine was somewhere below him in the cathedral, assuming her customary position beside Corbin Magnus and his retinue. Relatives and associates of the media magnate had been coming to the celestial castle day in and day out, ever since the abduction of Sylvia Magnus, adding their prayers to efforts to rescue the hostages.

Magnus covered all the bases, Bolan thought, appealing to higher forces as well as covert ones. But wherever the help came from, it was welcome.

That was one of the reasons why he was here.

Despite Bolan's initial reluctance to accept Victoria as liaison with Magnus, his opinion of her had changed for the better. Thanks to Hal Brognola.

The hard Fed had done some extensive digging into her background and come up with a solid dossier on her, pooling the information supplied by the Italian authorities with whatever the American spook net could uncover.

Corbin Magnus hadn't manufactured her background.

Victoria Celine looked as good on paper as she did in the flesh. She was cool under fire and had proved instrumental in a number of antiterrorist operations launched by the Carabinieri. According to Brognola's intel, the raven-haired beauty had infiltrated *brigatisti* cells throughout the country, helping to unravel the links in the terrorist underground.

She knew her business, whether she was working as part of a covert team or as a journalist. Since journalists often made the best intelligence agents, Victoria was definitely someone worth sharing information with.

Bolan looked at his watch.

He had another fifteen minutes before the meet. He scanned the square one more time, his black shades shielding his eyes from the late-morning sun.

Tucking his hands in his pockets and affecting the gait of a tourist exploring the walkways to heaven, Bolan killed a few more minutes atop the cathedral before heading down one of the stairways.

A warm dry breeze was blowing across the square, kicking up scattered bits of litter and ruffling the light black jacket that concealed Bolan's harnessed Beretta. He drifted over to one of the long bright red park benches on the edge of the square and took a seat next to an elderly white-haired man reading a copy of a Milanese tabloid. Wearing a faded but well-pressed suit, the man looked as if he'd been parked there since the benches first went up.

"Mind if I sit here?" Bolan asked.

"I'd mind if you didn't," the man replied, speaking in a northern dialect as he set down his newspaper.

Bolan smiled and before he knew it, found himself treated to a brief history of the man and his life in Milan. It appeared that without him, the city would have gone bankrupt decades earlier. The unofficial tour guide spoke with the voice of a schoolteacher, now and then sprinkling his soft-spoken speech with probing questions. This was a man who came here every day to read people as well as newspapers.

This was also a man who provided good cover. While Bolan maintained his end of the conversation, now and then inventing answers to match his persona as a tourist, he kept an eye on the cathedral steps and the steadily moving crowd.

Then he spotted Victoria Celine, veering off from the rest of Magnus's party as it climbed down the short wide steps of the cathedral's main entrance.

She was easy to spot, even without the bright white summer dress that clung to her abundant figure, making her tanned skin stand out even more from the light-colored cloth. There was a vibrancy in her step and a sense of urgency about her as she scanned the crowd for Bolan that marked her as a formidable woman. A woman who knew how to get things done . . . a woman used to getting her way.

She looked toward the bench where he waited, then quickly parted the waves of pedestrians, her high heels beating a stone tattoo as she neared him.

"Mike!" she said brightly, seeming genuinely pleased to see him.

He called out her name in return, then smiled broadly. It too was genuine. They'd agreed to stage their rendezvous as a date and that wasn't a hard thing to do, considering the attraction he felt toward her. He liked her looks and the way she carried herself.

As Bolan waved and stood, his unofficial tour guide picked up his newspaper, ruffled the pages and told the warrior what a lucky man he was to have a woman like that. Then he resumed reading his paper.

"Victoria," Bolan said, grabbing her hands as she reached out to him. Then, carrying out his cover, he kissed her on the cheek. "Good to see you."

"That's a nice surprise," she said, slipping her arm through his. "Last time we met, you were a—"

"Bit cautious," he interjected, enjoying the feel of her arm in his as they strolled across the square.

"A bit of a *bastard* is more like it."

"That too. Sometimes it comes with the territory."

"No argument there."

Bolan nodded. "Looks like we've covered a lot of the same territory."

She raised her eyebrows. "Sounds like you've been doing some homework."

"Yeah." He patted his pocket where a folded up sheet of paper was tucked away. "There's a few things we have to go over."

Victoria cocked her head. "You mean you didn't come here just to buy me a cup of coffee?"

"I wish it was that simple. But just like you didn't come here to go to church today, there's something else on my mind."

"A shame," she said brightly, giving him that same teasing gaze as the first time he met her. "What've you got for me?"

"A wish list," he said. "Maybe a hit list. A lot of names and places that might lead us to Sylvia Magnus."

"Let's talk about it over coffee." She nodded toward the north end of the plaza.

"Deal," Bolan said, ushering her toward Galleria Vittorio Emanuele. There beneath the glassed-in arcade of shops and cafés they could talk safely, covered by the steady noise from tourists, shoppers and locals who came to the gallery every day to gauge the cultural climate of Milan.

They walked past several crowded restaurants before grabbing an empty table at a narrow café sandwiched between an English-language bookstore and a leather shop.

After the waiter set a plate of pastries and cups of strong, freshly brewed black coffee in front of them, Bolan took out the sheet of paper from his jacket and passed it to her.

She unfolded it like a love note, then quickly scanned the names and places connected to Sinistra.

"Who's your source?" she asked.

"A temporary friend," Bolan replied.

"Why only temporary?"

"The only thing we've got in common is that we both want to see Amory Faust dead and Sinistra smashed."

"Is he one of us?"

"No," Bolan said, shaking his head. "Far from it. He's one of them."

Victoria raised her head, her eyes questioning him.

"Felix Giamante," he said, realizing they had to show some trust in each other. Besides, he had little doubt that Magnus hadn't already figured out who the players were.

Victoria blew steam away from her coffee, then sipped slowly before saying, "Felix Giamante is in the same business as Sinistra. If Faust didn't take Sylvia, it might have been him."

"Yeah, same business. And from what I saw, business was pretty good until he suddenly found himself at war with Amory Faust and Sinistra."

"Thanks to you."

"Thanks to me. That's why Giamante's only a temporary friend. When this is over, he'll want my head on the wall."

"And a Get-out-of-jail-free card."

Bolan shrugged. Deals were made with all kinds in this world. She knew it. He knew it. No one liked it. "Only for the duration. If we cross paths again after this is over and he's in the wrong..."

"Yes?"

"Then I correct him. Permanently."

"And in the meantime?"

"The deal is solid, and it's necessary. Giamante's in the same business as Sinistra. He uses the same tactics. And," Bolan said, tapping on the list she'd spread out on the table, "he has the kind of contacts and know-how that gives us this."

Victoria smoothed out the list, running her finger down the names. "It does look complete," she said. "And it looks familiar. A regular *Who's Who* of the underworld."

"Then he's not running a scam on us."

"No. I'd say Giamante's wish list is right on target. Of course, he's probably loaded the list with a few of his long-term enemies who have nothing to do with Sinistra and he hopes we take them down. They should be easy enough to spot. The others can all be put under a microscope.''

''Right,'' Bolan said. ''Or a hammer.''

She laughed. ''Whatever works.''

He pointed out a few of the names on the bottom of the list. Right after the hoods and killers were the lawyers and bankers who helped the kidnap industry thrive. They laundered the money, set up front companies, administered legal dead-drops and courier services, established hidden accounts for the clans to draw upon. ''I'm going to pay a few calls to the money-handlers, see what I can dig up from these paragons of virtue.''

Victoria smiled at him and dropped her hand over his. ''I understand you can be quite persuasive at times.''

''Like you said—whatever works.''

''We'll have to meet again,'' she said. ''To compare notes.''

''Another date?''

''Yes.''

Bolan leaned back in the chair, studying Victoria—the black hair that swept down to her bare rounded shoulders, the way she leaned forward, subtly presenting a glimpse of her full cleavage. And for a moment Bolan was convinced that she really did want a date. Not a rendezvous. Not a chance to compare notes. But a chance for something more.

A chance he would gladly take.

"A date it is," he agreed. "But before we go, let's go over the list again."

"Always business with you," she chided.

"You live longer that way."

"You're right. Longer but duller." Once again Victoria teased him with her eyes. Then she got down to business, giving him a rundown of some of the names and the sites on the list, pointing out the most probable targets and the most dangerous. Then they planned on how they would go about toppling an underworld empire.

Bolan paid the check, taking Victoria's hand as they walked back into the glassed-in arcade. As they neared the Piazza del Duomo, he said, "You sure this isn't too down-to-earth for you?"

"What do you mean?"

"You know," Bolan said. "These people and places you're going to investigate. They must seem so mundane to you after all of the other scoops you've had."

"What are you talking about?"

"None of them are off-planet."

She smacked him on the arm. "You've been doing a bit too much homework."

Among Victoria Celine's long list of publications were several of the more outré magazines and tabloids under the Magnus umbrella. She'd covered stories about UFOs hovering above NATO bases in Italy. Bigfoot in the Alps. Werewolves. Ghosts. Everything but an Elvis sighting at the Vatican.

"Magnus wanted me to get around," she explained. "To get known. And to deal with every level of society. That's why I did those stories. I don't believe in that nonsense."

"Don't worry," Bolan said. "Your secret's safe with me." Then he left her in the square, armed with a list of killers and kidnappers he'd brought to their first date.

9

The villa was nestled in the foothills of the Alps, midway between the medieval walled town of Bergamo and Val Brembana. Like many of the isolated villas along the stretch of road veering away from the S 470 into the lake district, it sat on a small peak surrounded by cypress groves and mulberry bushes.

It looked very peaceful to Victoria Celine, who watched it through the infrared eyes of the Smith & Wesson scope attached to her 35 mm camera.

Now that the caravan of troops had left, there were only a few men inside the villa. If she hadn't been watching all day and part of the night from her observation post in the woods, she might have thought they were innocent.

But she'd taken too many shots through the tripod-mounted long-range lens to dismiss the villa as a potential Sinistra safehouse. Too many hard-looking men had called it home.

Instinct told her the site was hot and that Giamante's people had delivered the goods. They'd used their contacts to ferret out another Sinistra strong-hold.

Instinct also told her that it was time for her to leave the area. Victoria had pressed her luck enough already, moving from site to site to get photos from as many angles as possible. Although she was dressed in dark green khakis and a black-and-green scarf streaked with woodland camouflage colors, there was always a chance she'd been seen.

A moment later the chance became reality when she heard the rustle of branches slashing through the air.

She turned and faced a forest of darkness, glimpsing a shadow moving behind her. But it was only an afterimage. The shadow came either from her mind or from an intruder.

Then she heard footsteps off to her left. The sound ended abruptly after attracting her attention.

Victoria tensed and stood perfectly still. Like a fawn hoping to avoid a predator, she tried to pin-point her stalker's hiding place before choosing her escape route.

Then she sprang up suddenly from the ground, heart jumping in her chest, blood pounding in her ears as a curtain of fear dropped over her eyes and made every shadow look menacing. But she had no choice anymore. She had to make a break for it.

The camera toppled to the ground, the tripod snaring her feet in her panic and tripping her up as she stumbled for the safety of the woods. She took two quick steps before she fell into an iron-hard grasp that lifted her off her feet and swung her around in a circle.

Like a dance, she thought.

A dance of the dead.

Her captor grunted as he closed in on her. She kicked out as hard as she could with her heel, her foot glancing off a rock-solid thigh.

Victoria tried once again, this time completely missing her target. And still she was held in the painful grip.

She started to scream, then checked herself when she finally deciphered the calming voice that had been talking to her all along. It was the voice of a friend.

It was Belasko.

"Easy," he repeated in a soothing tone. "It's me. There's nothing to worry about."

"I know it's you!" she hissed, twisting her wrists sharply to break free of his grip. "What I want to know is why you're here. Are you following me?" Despite her protests, relief flooded through her.

"No. We're following the same targets. We just happen to be on the same track."

She looked up at the tall man in black, his face streaked with shadowy camouflage, his eyes glinting in the moonlight like a creature on the prowl. She shuddered, realizing that this was the way he really was. This was the true man behind all of the masks she'd seen him wear.

He wasn't a negotiator, nor a diplomat.

He was a hunter, and he had scented his prey out here in the dark and the cold. This was his arena.

"Didn't you trust me to check them out myself?" she asked.

"Yeah, I did. That was the problem. I knew you'd come here alone and take a lot of risks to get the answers I wanted."

"So why did you come?"

He paused for a moment, then said, "Too much blood has already been shed on my account. I don't want to see any more innocents get hurt."

"I can take care of myself," she snapped. "I've been doing that for years now. Years before *you* came along."

"I know. You're pretty good, Victoria—almost good enough to escape detection."

Victoria backed away from him, the anger and fear slowly fading as she realized the truth in what he was saying. Like him, she had dressed to blend in with the countryside. And that had helped her escape detection from the men in the villa. But not from him.

And that made her feel better in a way. After all, he was on her side.

"Looks like our temporary friend came through for us," he said, nodding toward the house on the peak.

"That's the way I see it. Giamante gave us some solid leads."

"More than leads," Bolan told her. "This is the real thing. A hard site. Staging area for Sinistra operations. Maybe something more."

"Like what?"

"Like a place where they keep prisoners. Of all the places I checked out on Giamante's list, this one looks like the best. And now we've got to make sure."

"How?"

The warrior nodded toward the hilltop aerie. "I'll go and ask them."

"You expect them to talk?"

"Yeah," the warrior replied. "I expect them to tell me anything I want them to. It's all in the way you ask."

Victoria stiffened from an unseen chill that swept over her. It came from the inside, from the gut. She'd been on covert operations before, but it was usually in an undercover or support role. This was rapidly escalating into wet work.

"We've got to make sure," she said. "What if we're wrong? What if it's just a group of innocent people—"

"It's not."

"How can you be sure?"

"Come over here and see for yourself."

She followed his voice deep into the woods, deep into the vine-covered shadows. They hurried through the splintered streams of moonlight that fell upon the forest bed—and upon the bulky form lying on the ground.

It was a man, stretched out flat on his back. A dark liquid necklace streamed onto his shirt, the blood forming a small gruesome pond by the side of his head.

"Who is it?"

"He's the man who was about to kill you," said the man in black, "with this." He stepped forward and kicked at an automatic rifle with his foot.

"Oh God."

"Yeah," he said. " 'Oh God' is right. You came *this* close to having a face-to-face with him." He gestured with a flick of his hand across his throat. "I had no choice. He was getting ready to take you out."

Victoria shook her head. "I didn't even hear a thing. I didn't even know he was out here."

"He was patrolling the perimeter. Circled around making hardly a sound. Walked right by me and didn't see a thing. Then he zeroed in on you."

"I'm glad you're here."

"Me too," Bolan said. Then he was gone.

THE EXECUTIONER ZIGZAGGED up the hillside, stopping now and then to scan the villa with the small Spylux Personal Night Scope.

One man walked outside the main house, cradling a submachine gun in his beefy hands. He kept well outside the rim of light from the illuminated windows. But he still wasn't hidden. Through the night scope, his intensified image looked like a ghost.

A second guard sat on the porch near one of the sheds that flanked the house. This man was also armed, holding an automatic rifle at the ready. Both were waiting for the return of the man who had gone out to patrol the grounds.

A man who would never return.

Something had obviously spooked them. Maybe they had actually spotted Victoria and sent the hardman out to find her. Or it could be the unsettling mountain silence that provoked a random tour of the perimeter.

But whatever it was, Bolan was going to make sure they didn't know about him until it was too late.

He had no doubt that this was a Sinistra site. Giamante had pinpointed it, and Bolan had scoped it out, seeing some familiar faces that matched some of the Sinistra mug shots he'd scanned in Brognola's temporary headquarters in Milan.

And then there was the man on patrol. He'd drawn a bead on an unarmed woman, then smiled. He was either going in for the kill, or he was going to have some fun with his victim first. A moonlight prize.

Innocent men didn't stalk unarmed women.

Bolan had seen too many of his kind before to doubt the outcome. And so he'd changed it with a quick slash of a combat knife.

As the Executioner neared the closer Sinistra gunman, he came to a complete stop and listened intently for voices from within the house.

Silence.

The two gunners outside the house were past the point of conversation. They were nervous, and waited impatiently for the return of the other man. Or for an attack. They were traversing a no-man's-land of the mind, with every passing second offering a different answer. Was their comrade safe and on the way back now? Or had he been hit somewhere in the woods?

Bolan knifed through the trees, then stepped out into the open. Still hidden by the shadows, he moved as stealthily as a summer night's breeze.

If he made a sound it might be his last.

But he had no choice. He wanted to take one of them alive, which meant he had to get close to the guard standing in the shadows. Close enough to take him down after he terminated the other threat.

Bolan pressed the wire stock of the Beretta 93-R against his shoulder, swinging the suppressed barrel toward the man whom fate had chosen to receive a 9 mm message about the Executioner's decision.

He exhaled and pulled the trigger.

The man on the porch toppled back, gasping in surprise. His rifle rolled harmlessly to the porch while a dark hole in his neck dribbled blood.

The other guard jerked his head over his shoulder, trying to see what had happened.

Bolan closed the gap, sprinting across the ten feet that separated them and thumping a hammer fist into the back of the gunman's skull.

The Sinistra guard reacted at the last second, instinct finally screaming at him to go into action. He tried to unleash a back kick, but Bolan's strike derailed him in the middle of the effort. The kick died quickly and his foot dropped harmlessly back to the ground in a stumbling half step.

The hammer fist had stunned him, toppling him forward in a jerky motion.

The Executioner darted after his prey. He planted his left foot on the ground, then unleashed a round-house kick that drilled into the gunner's chest like a baseball bat, the hard ridge of bone smashing into him with a dull thud.

The impact of the blow caved in the last shred of resistance and laid the man out flat on the ground, facedown.

Crouching beside the hardman, Bolan quickly tore away the guy's submachine gun, which had dropped onto the ground, and told him he had questions that needed answers.

The man fought to regain his breath.

He was young, his hair long and wild, his face white with fear, his voice quaking with panic as he talked a mile a minute. Until now, his work for Sinistra had always been one-way. He wasn't used to people who fought back. Or people who struck first.

"Speak slowly!" Bolan demanded in Italian, as the words burst from the guard in an unintelligible flood.

The man nodded, then slowed down, explaining that he didn't know anything. He was just here for the night, called up to watch over things. He didn't know why. He didn't really know anyone in the group and only happened to be there, a good soldier doing his job.

It was a story Bolan had heard a hundred times before.

"That's not what I want to hear," the warrior growled, pressing the barrel of the Beretta against the man's temple. "Keep it up and you really won't know anything." He flicked the selector to 3-round burst.

"Okay," the sentry gasped, nodding his head, one side of his face pressed into the dirt.

"How many people inside?" Bolan asked.

"None."

"Why?"

"We are the only ones left."

"Where's everyone else?"

"I don't know."

"Guess," Bolan suggested.

The man clammed up. He either had no more knowledge or something frightened him even worse than the barrel of the Beretta—certain death at the hands of Sinistra. A certain and slow death.

Bolan fished out a nylon cord from a pocket of his combat vest, wrapped it around the man's wrists and sealed the lightweight cuffs with a quick snap. "On your feet," he said, tugging the man until he scrambled into an upright position.

Then he checked the house.

It was as his prisoner had said, and as his recon had indicated. Empty.

The Executioner inspected the shed on the right of the house, flicking on a battery-operated lantern and running the dust-filled light beam over the worn wood. He paused, then moved the beam toward the middle of the shed where there was an outline on the floor.

He flashed the beam into his prisoner's face.

"Is this where they were kept?" Bolan demanded.

The man cowered but remained silent.

Bolan aimed the Beretta and pulled the trigger.

The Sinistra gunman screamed, then caught himself in midshriek as he realized he was still alive. His world hadn't come to an end. And there was still a chance to reverse the decision he made to go down fighting.

"My aim gets better," Bolan warned, stepping closer. "This time's for real. This time's forever."

"All right," the man said. "They were here."

"Who?"

"The Magnus girl. She was in this one."

"Was she hurt?"

The man looked up at the Beretta, as if he were weighing the gun barrel in his decision. Finally he shook his head. "No, she was not hurt. Not intentionally. But she was tired, hungry. Frightened. It's only natural. That is how they are kept."

"You speak from experience."

He shrugged. "You do not want me to lie, so I'm telling you what it was like."

"What about her fiancé?"

He smiled. "The brave one. They kept him in the other shed. Private accommodations, you see. He is no longer pretty to look at, but he is basically unharmed."

"What did they do to him?"

"Condorri brought it on himself. He fought every chance he got. That one thinks he is Hercules."

Bolan took his prisoner into the shed that flanked the other side of the house, and there saw the signs of a one-sided struggle. The signs of a man beaten. There was dried blood on the floor and blood on the walls.

"He's still alive?"

"Like I said, the man's in rough shape, but nothing permanent. He only got hurt because of the way he acted."

"What was that?"

"He fought back against Faust, and no one does that. No one. So he got what was coming to him."

"Sounds like you're a firm believer in justice," Bolan said.

The Sinistra gunner ignored the remark.

Bolan flashed the light on the blood marks again. They'd come so close. The leads had checked out. Sylvia and Giancarlo had been here, almost in their grasp. But now Sinistra was on the move, lessening their chances of discovery.

The hostages had probably been moved several times already, Bolan thought. This was just the latest stop on the underground express.

Sinistra had played it smart, keeping both of the abductees relatively close to where they'd been kidnapped, which cut down the chance of being discovered. It also threw the authorities off guard since many of them expected the kidnappers to take their victims to the south.

"There still might be a chance for justice," Bolan said, aiming the Beretta at the center of the man's forehead. "We're not done yet."

"What else do you want?"

"Where did they take them?" Bolan said.

"I don't know. I have no idea—"

"Give it your best shot," Bolan suggested, "or I will."

The Sinistra captive shook his head, then he spoke so softly that Bolan couldn't hear him. It was almost as if the man were afraid to speak in more than a whisper.

"Where?" Bolan asked, lowering his voice and consequently the man's tension level at the same time.

"Maggiore."

"The lake?"

"Yes."

"Whereabouts?" Bolan demanded. "That's a lot of territory to cover."

"That's all I know," the man said. "Only because I overheard some of them talking about it. They told me nothing. Just to stay put until I was needed. Then they all went to Lake Maggiore." His voice grew bitter as he added, "And left us here to die."

"No. You talked. For that, you'll live."

The man shook his head slowly. "You're wrong. I talked. And for *that* I will die."

"In that case," Bolan said, "talk some more. When I'm convinced you've told me everything, you're free to go."

"My people will still come after me."

"Yeah, they probably will. But if you talk fast enough, you'll get a good head start."

The Sinistra gunman looked at the Beretta 93-R, then at the stony eyes of the Executioner.

And there he saw the promise of sudden death.

So he talked, filling in all that he could about the underworld operation of Amory Faust, spilling out names of friends and enemies alike, and a list of crimes and conquests he'd carried out for the clan.

Finally he fell silent.

THREE HOURS LATER, Bolan stood behind Victoria Celine in the windowless photo studio she'd built on one side of her top-floor flat on Via Brera in the old quarter of Milan. Blowups of fashion spreads and portrait shots lined the walls, presenting a brightly colored history of the people and stories she'd covered in her role as a photojournalist over the past ten years. Models, ministers and wide-eyed yeti hunters stood side by side in all of their errant glory. Glossy magazine covers shared spaced with the tabloid headlines.

The walls were an unofficial résumé of her life with Corbin Magnus, both during and after his Carabinieri days. There was a lot more sensitive material in the stacks of binders and files that filled up every square inch of available space. Victoria's place on Via Brera was a one-woman intelligence bank, full of surveillance files and photos she'd amassed on covert operations.

At the moment she was preparing to add more to them, swishing her hands softly in a transparent solution that filled a shallow developing tray. Like a gypsy telling fortunes, she stared hard at the sheets that came to life in her hands, images of hard-faced men appearing in slow motion.

When the photographs were clear enough to distinguish, she clipped them to the drying rack where they hung like glossy branches on a tree.

A tree of evil.

For the faces belonged to men of Sinistra—gunmen, drivers, killers, thugs. The whole family tree.

By now Bolan was familiar with many of the Sinistra clan from the mug shots he'd been studying since his arrival in Milan. The faces and names were etched in his memory, flashing into his mind whenever he summoned them. It was one more skill that helped him beat the odds over the years. He had to be able to pick out a face at a moment's notice and decide if it was friend or foe.

Right now he was looking at a familiar face.

"I've seen this one before," Bolan said, tapping the latest face she'd hung on the photo tree.

The photograph showed a bald-domed heavy with a thick walrus mustache. The man was wide in the shoulders and had tree-stump legs. There was little fat on him, just a mountain of muscle.

Victoria's shot had captured him while he was directing two other Sinistra men who were moving around the back of a van that was backed up to the shed on the right side of the house.

"Where do you know him from?" Victoria asked.

"He's the one who got away," Bolan replied, thinking back to the night of his attack on the first Sinistra stronghold with his reluctant ally Felix Giamante.

He told her about the strongman who'd thrown himself out the window during the firefight, the man who regrouped the Sinistra gunners and led them on a pursuit through the woods.

"He fits the bill," Victoria said. "His name is Clement Lacazino."

"You know him, too?"

"I know of him," she corrected. "His nickname is Locozino. He is a suspected enforcer with long-established ties to the kidnap trade."

"And?"

"The key word is 'suspected,'" she said. "No convictions yet, though he's been implicated in several robberies and assaults. After the first few witnesses against him vanished, no one ever dared testify against him. They always seemed to have a lapse of memory when it came to trial. Or it would suddenly turn out to be a case of mistaken identity."

"We can't really blame them," Bolan said. "The law doesn't protect them. Hell, most of the time the law doesn't get involved until there's a civilian stretched out on the ground. Even then they don't always go after the perps. It's as bad in my country as it is in yours. It's the same wherever people don't make a stand."

She nodded, brushing a few strands of hair from her forehead as she stared him straight in the eye. "People like us, you mean."

"People like us."

Bolan felt a pull toward her. There was something in her dark eyes that reached out to him, something in her voice, in the stillness of the late hour they'd found themselves sharing. Most of the other houses in the quarter were silent and blacked out for the night, their occupants with normal lives to wake to in the morning.

But Bolan and Victoria had left that kind of life far behind them. They lived their lives behind curtains, putting on masks for the public while they carried out their true missions. Only rarely could they remove those masks.

Now was such a time.

For them the night was just beginning. There were more photos to study, more intel to go over—names, places, probabilities, risks, logistics for the search of Lake Maggiore.

Each would have to follow up the initial reports they'd already made to their people with a more detailed briefing about this night's operation, which Magnus's media outlets would play up as the latest battle in the hit-and-run war between rival bands of L'Anonima Sequestri.

But that could wait.

He stepped forward, still holding on to Victoria's green-eyed gaze, reading her mind and her soul, then her body as she closed the gap between them.

Bolan snared his arms around her, caressing the small of her back and smelling the lilac scent of the long black hair that brushed against him.

She turned her head up and exposed her neck, a soft fountain of flesh for his mouth.

The buttons of her khaki shirt were easily undone as his hand swept steadily downward, revealing another kind of camouflage. Her black brassiere was sheer and silky, clinging to her like frosting beneath his fingertips.

She groaned softly and pressed against him. As the temperature rose, her eyes closed and her lips turned downward.

Bolan shed his night-black gear and stepped closer to her, his hands trailing her hips, his mouth tracing a path over her bare breasts.

She spoke his name.

His false name.

But it didn't matter. The sound was real. Mike or Mack—it was all the same now. What mattered was the warm hush of her breath against his shoulder, the shuddering of her body and the clinging of her fingernails as she pulled him closer.

Gradually they moved to the rear of the studio and through the door that led to her bedroom. She sat on the edge of the bed, her dark hair shading part of her face while moonlight illuminated her body.

Bolan's shadow passed in front of the moonlight, and a moment later their entwined bodies fell onto the wide bed.

Then the two of them began condensing a lifetime into a nighttime.

IN THE MORNING Mack Bolan studied the contours of Lake Maggiore on a large-scale map spread out on a worktable in Victoria's studio. Maggiore was a mirror-smooth jewel in the middle of Italy's lake country, with more than a hundred miles of shoreline braced by undulating hills and forests, island castles, ruins, resorts and picturesque villages. A good portion of the lake was at least two miles wide. There was plenty of green between the resort areas and small villages, connected by roads.

A lot of wild country to hide in, Bolan thought, and a lot to search through.

Making it even more difficult was the fact that the northern part of the lake stretched well inside Switzerland's border.

It would be a delicate situation if they had to go into Switzerland. But Magnus was getting prepared to do whatever he had to do. According to Victoria, Magnus had been carefully vetting his team of special forces, assembling a trusted core ready to go into action, while at the same time isolating a couple of Carabinieri suspects they believed might be working in tandem with Sinistra.

Sinistra was on the move and that meant he had to stay on the move. But he needed more intel.

So far all the Executioner had to go on was the word of a captive Sinistra gunman, a lower-echelon bandit who was bargaining for his life. A man in that condition would give up information even if he had to manufacture it.

Other possibilities came to mind. What if the man had been intentionally misled? What if Lake Maggiore was just a stop on the way to the real location?

The new Sinistra safehouse could be at any of the small villages just a few miles away from the lake. They could be anywhere, and that meant that Bolan would have to cover a lot of ground before he could narrow down the search.

He scanned the map one more time, subconsciously looking for the X that marked the spot.

If only it were that easy, Bolan thought, using a sixth sense for target acquisition. His instinct told him it was time to get some more help. Even if that help needed some encouragement.

He would hit Maggiore soon enough. But first he had to make a slight detour.

He'd hit the illegal arm of Sinistra wherever possible.

Now it was time to twist the legal one.

10

The blond-haired receptionist was used to unusual demands from some of the clients who visited the outwardly staid offices of the Milan branch of Peregrine Internationale.

Located just off Piazza Mercanti, the narrow two-story building was sandwiched between old granite-and-glass banks that looked like ornate churches built for the worship of money.

Peregrine was mostly involved in trading and investments, real-estate and corporate financing. But it was also involved in the kind of activities that brought men like the man in the black jacket to their door. No appointment. No small talk. Just business.

Money business.

He wanted to see Pascal Quillon, the chief executive officer of Peregrine, and he wanted to see him now.

"I'll give him your name."

"No. I'll give it to him. Personally."

"I see." Dressed primly in starched white blouse and a black ribbon tie with a round onyx tie clasp, the woman was the picture of legitimacy. But the fact that she worked for Peregrine meant she was as legitimate as the exquisitely framed Botticelli and Caravaggio knockoffs adorning the walls behind her.

She studied him closely, categorizing him like she did everyone who walked into the office. He was lean and fit, dressed well if a bit darkly, and there was a look in his eyes that she didn't see often. This man wouldn't be put off from anything. Anywhere. Anytime.

He was the type her boss referred to as "hard men with hard currency." They didn't like people to know where they got their money from and where that money went. That was where Pascal Quillon came in.

"I'd appreciate it if you could hurry things up," the man said, flashing a thin smile that warned her not to turn her back on him. "I've got other appointments to make today."

She smiled back at him. "We can go as fast as you like. Or as slow. It's up to you. But before we go a step further, I need to have a name."

"He'll see me."

"Maybe he will," she replied. "But not without a name." She risked a defiant look.

"I'd like to keep mine confidential, just between me and Signore Quillon," he said. "Until then, how about a name of a mutual friend?"

"Yes," she said, relief flooding her voice. "That will be fine. This friend's name is—"

"Felix."

"Last name?"

He shook his head again. "Your superior will know. Try it out on him."

"Very well."

She left her desk, tapped softly on the door and opened it halfway. She carried on a hushed conversation with Pascal Quillon, then returned to her desk.

"He'll see you now."

"Wonderful."

The woman led him to the inner office, watching him every step of the way with a mixture of caution and attraction mingled in her gaze.

Pascal Quillon stood behind a long and wide marble-inlaid desk that lent a rock-solid appearance to his office. His silver hair was immaculately groomed, every hair in place. And though he wore the funeral-black suit of a banker, he had the eyes of a gambler.

Otherwise, he wouldn't have granted an interview to the man who introduced himself as Michael Belasko.

After shaking hands, Quillon settled his potential client in a black leather chair facing his desk. Then he sat behind his desk with the countenance of a priest about to hear confession and exact a healthy commission as penance. "Now we can talk."

"Sorry for coming here on short notice."

"I pride myself on cutting through red tape," Quillon said. "In my business you must be available at all times."

"That's what I was told."

The broker nodded. "Yes. Uh, I understand that Felix recommended me. Just to make sure we are talking about the same man, when you say 'Felix,' of course you mean Felix . . ."

"Giamante."

Quillon nodded his benediction. "Right. We've worked together on a number of projects in the past. Usually in matters such as this he would let me know beforehand."

"He's kind of involved at the moment. There's a certain situation demanding all of his time. He said it wouldn't be a problem." He leaned forward in the leather chair, pushing his hands up on the well-cushioned arms. "If it is, then I'll take my leave now."

"No, no, please," Quillon said. "I can always contact him later. I just mention it to show you how cautious we are with our clientele. Since we can't always work through the, eh, regular channels, names and reputations are important in this business. Now if you could tell me how you know Felix?"

"Very well," he said. "We work together."

Quillon nodded again and leaned forward over his desk, scenting the money coming his way. "For our immediate purposes I'll need to know exactly what you require." He paused, smiling, and said, "And when you require it."

Bolan pinned him with an unwavering gaze. "I require a hell of a lot, and I require it today."

"That can be quite costly, you understand."

"Oh yeah," Bolan said. "I understand perfectly the stakes involved. I'll do whatever it takes."

"Good. As long as we understand each other I believe we can do business together. I'm sure your references will check out. In the meantime we can start setting up an apparatus." Bolan nodded and smiled. Men like Pascal Quillon always had just the right words to cover up what was really going on. They used the same terminology for underworld deals as they did for their aboveground work. Apparatus, Bolan thought. Dummy corporations. Secret funds. Untouchable assets.

"Now," Quillon said. "What exactly are you looking for?"

"A magician," the Executioner replied.

"Oh?"

"Someone who can make money vanish like that," he said, snapping his fingers. "And of course, someone who can make it appear again just as fast when it is needed. That same someone should be able to make it impossible to trace."

The money-handler smiled knowingly. "A bit of illusion is what you need. Some magic words, let us say, the names of front companies. Some magic boxes to hide this money until it is needed. Yes. This kind of thing can be done with my contacts up north.''

''The Swiss.''

''Exactly,'' Quillon said. ''I work with some of the most reputable bankers in Zurich.''

''Are they still safe?'' he asked. ''From what I've heard, they've become a bit too free with their information.''

''To some extent,'' Quillon admitted. ''Though there have been some changes in recent years, with more and more governmental snooping into financial affairs, there are still a number of good men who know how to handle certain special accounts. Believe me, they are most efficient in these matters. And most discreet.''

''I'm sure they are,'' Bolan said. ''But I may need some more magic. Someone who can provide names. Paperwork. Passports.''

Quillon shrugged. ''As you know, I am the man to see for the financial end of it. There are others who can handle these additional needs of yours.''

''Can you provide references?''

''Perhaps that could be arranged.''

''For a commission, of course.''

''Yes, as I say, I could pass a word here or there. And then you could work things out with the others. But my own expertise lies with the money side of it. Naturally it is only worthwhile if we handle substantial amounts.''

Bolan drew back as if he were insulted. "Naturally," he said. "If you think I'm wasting your time, then I'll try to find someone else—"

"No, please do not misunderstand me," Quillon said hastily. "I'm sure the figure you have in mind will be sufficient. Otherwise Felix would not have sent you here." The silver-haired, silver-tongued banker clasped his hands together like a supplicant, almost pleading for the money to come his way.

"All right," Bolan said. "You've convinced me that you're the one I'm looking for. The man who can handle the kind of matters I'm interested in."

Quillon nodded. His hands dropped to his desktop, then swept inward as if he were raking in money across the table. "We all have our specialties."

"Yes, that we do," Bolan agreed. "And my specialty is..." He lowered his voice as if he were about to reveal a great secret.

"Yes?" Quillon asked, leaning forward politely.

The Executioner reached inside his jacket and withdrew the silenced Beretta 93-R. "My specialty is killing people."

The blood drained from Quillon's face. He planted his hands palm-down on the desk, anchoring himself in fear.

The banker had made a number of enemies in his career. He'd made an equal number of friends. Both sides might have reason to have him silenced. Secrets lasted longer when they were only held by dead men.

The man was frozen in place.

"I only kill people who get in my way," Bolan said, idly training the gun on him. "People who do not give me the help I expect from them. Do you understand?"

Quillon nodded rapidly, a puppet whose strings could be cut at any moment by the hard-eyed man facing him. "Yes, but—but you couldn't get away with this," he stuttered, clutching at his rapidly dwindling hopes. "My assistant is right outside that door. She'll hear—"

Bolan waved the barrel of the Beretta toward the closed door. "She's no problem. This has more than one bullet."

"What do you want from me? If it's money, we never have much actual currency on hand."

"I want something a lot more valuable than that. I want some truth."

Quillon's eyes narrowed, seeing that there were some odds he could play. The gambling spark returned to his eyes. "Truth is a scarce commodity in this business."

"Damned near obsolete," Bolan agreed, holding the Beretta steady on Quillon and letting the menacing black barrel do the talking for him.

"What do you want?"

"I want a man who calls himself Amory Faust," the warrior replied. "I understand that you've done a lot of business with him. Sinistra business."

"Never heard of him," Quillon protested, shaking his head in abject sorrow. It was the pose of a man who wished to help but couldn't. "Or Sinistra—"

Bolan sprang across the wide desk in a blur, pressing the barrel of the Beretta into Quillon's forehead. "Then I guess I'd better cut my losses here and now."

The banker's eyes rose slowly, drawn like magnets to the deadly iron. The metal weighed heavily on the silver-haired fixer. No quick lies spilled from his lips. He knew that death was a very real dividend if he did the wrong thing.

The Executioner knew he was the kind of man Amory Faust would use, but there was no guarantee he was the right one. Felix Giamante had used Quillon in the past. So did many others in the underworld who'd come into a lot of money real fast and had to hide it just as fast.

Such things were impossible without the help of semilegal fixers like Quillon.

Quillon was the third fixer Bolan had targeted for a get-acquainted session. The other two had also been crooked and at one time or another had also helped Felix Giamante handle his finances. But neither of them had been the crook in question, the money man who helped manage Amory Faust's clandestine fortune.

Both of those men were still alive, if a bit shaken up. In the future they might be a bit more cautious about working on the wrong side of the law.

Bolan sensed he had hit the jackpot with Quillon. The man was turning pale with fear. Obviously the man was guilty of something. But did it involve Amory Faust?

"Like I told your assistant out there," Bolan said, "I've got some more appointments to keep. Unless you start talking real soon, I'm afraid I'll have to close your account."

"I can't talk like this," he replied, slowly raising his hand and pointing at the Beretta. "I can't think."

"So think." Bolan stepped back, giving him room to breathe.

Quillon wiped the back of his hand across his forehead, then smoothed his silver hair. "My dealings with all of my clients are kept quite confidential," he said. "Such relationships are based on trust."

"Such relationships can be fatal."

"What is it you want?"

"As I told you before, I have certain needs. I need to find Amory Faust."

The banker threw up his hands. "What can I do? It is out of my hands. I don't know where he is, or what he's done."

"You know where he might be," Bolan said. "You know where his money is hidden. My guess is you set up a few cutouts for him. Fancy companies with fancy stationery and an imaginary board of directors. Things like that. Things that can be traced.''

Quillon seemed to be searching for courage to defy him, but couldn't find it. The man was crooked, but he was easily steered if you knew what buttons to push, what triggers to pull.

"What is this to you?" he asked. "You're not the police. You're not one of us. What gives you the right to interfere?"

"I take the right," Bolan said. "I take back the rights that people like you have taken away."

"But I'm just a middleman. I'm not responsible for how these people get their money."

"But you are. You make it possible for them to hide their money, to hide themselves. They know if they commit the crime, you'll always be there to help them in their hour of need. For a percentage, of course."

"You can't do this," Quillon protested. "I have my rights."

"Not as long as I'm here. What you have is five minutes. Unless you use them wisely, I suggest you make out a will."

"You put me in an impossible position—"

"Five minutes," Bolan repeated, "to decide whether you'll be staying here, or the hereafter."

"If word gets out about this I am a dead man."

"Let me explain something to you. You think because you hide behind legitimate businesses, because you deal with well-dressed bankers in well-dressed suits, that you are removed from the battle-field.''

Quillon nodded slowly as if he agreed with the lame philosophy. As long as he didn't pull the trigger, as long as he didn't organize the crime, then it wasn't his fault what happened or where the money came from.

''You close your eyes and take your cut, then you think you are finished. I'm here to tell you that the battlefield is where I decide to take it. And right now I'm taking it to you.''

Quillon looked at the ceiling as if he were seeking help from some god above—the god of corrupt bankers. The patron saint of secondhand killers.

Then he looked at Bolan again, his eyes searching for some clue, some sign that this might be a bluff.

''I've done this before,'' the Executioner said.

''What?''

''Seen the look in a man's eyes when he's wondering if I'm going to kill him or not.''

''Yes?''

''And I've seen the look in that man's eyes when he realizes it's too late because I've made up my mind to kill him.''

''All right!'' Quillon shouted. ''All right, I'll tell you. But this must remain confidential.''

''Just between you and me,'' Bolan promised. ''Tell me what I want and I'll go my way.''

That was the key that unlocked Quillon's black soul. The banker spoke rapidly. He had an amazing command of detail, combining the precision of a bookkeeper with the soul of a Sinistra paymaster. He had worked with Amory Faust, he admitted. He didn't know where Faust was now or what he did with the money, but he knew how Faust drew his accounts.

There was a dummy corporation set up with branch offices in Switzerland and Liechtenstein. The mother corporation diverted funds to a number of subsidiary companies that Faust could draw upon as needed, using a number of names that supposedly made up the board of directors.

It was a corporate shell game. One company fed funds to another company and created a paper trail that was almost impossible to follow—unless you had the right resources at hand. Like a joint U.S. and Italian covert task force that had been waiting for the opportunity to strike.

Bolan listened carefully to the song of the Sinistra banker, now and then questioning the man, but most of the time letting him weave his own tale of intrigue and deception as he painted a portrait of Amory Faust's covert corporation, AmicusCo.

"I have one more favor to ask," Bolan said when Quillon was finished.

"Yes?"

"If Faust gets in touch with you for any reason, give me a call." He grabbed a sheet of notepaper from a memo pad on Quillon's desk and wrote down one of the untraceable phone lines set up by the U.S.

consulate for messages from "friends" like Pascal Quillon.

The banker took the paper and looked at the number, but didn't seem too enthused.

"If Faust gets in touch with you, make the call and it just might save a life. Yours."

"All right," Quillon said. "I'll call."

11

A hard rain was falling when the Executioner eased the green Fiat down the alley between the fortress-like walls of the apartment complex near the consulate on Piazza del Repubblica.

The windshield wipers beat a steady tattoo on the glass, drumming in counterpoint to the jangling pop music playing on the car radio.

Though the U.S. Embassy was in Rome, in recent years the covert community had been concentrating more and more on Milan since it was rapidly becoming the nerve center of Italy, the place where the money and machinery of commerce flowed.

That meant the consulate in Milan had virtually unlimited resources at its disposal, currently tapped by Hal Brognola who'd sent out a call for Bolan.

The call had reached the warrior at Victoria Celine's place. He'd been using it as a base of operations the past few days. They worked well together, and in those rare moments when time allowed, they played well together.

Bolan had passed word to Felix Giamante and company to concentrate their efforts on the Lake Maggiore region and see what they could dig up.

The same word had gone out to select units of the Carabinieri and commando squads from the Nucleo Operativo Centrale di Sicurezza, otherwise known as NOCS.

Also joining the search from the American side was a network of official and unofficial operatives under the guiding hand of Hal Brognola.

The Executioner parked the Fiat next to a sporty all-terrain vehicle that was all wheels and no chassis, then hurried down the shadowed corridor between the gray stone buildings, the heavy rain beating down on the hood of his slicker. Two security guards met him at the door and waved him through. By now he was a familiar sight in the complex.

A rush of cold air swept over him as he walked down the marble corridor. The air-conditioning was going full tilt. Despite the brief and sudden rain, a sweltering and humid haze hung over the city.

As Bolan walked down the hallways he noticed a steady flurry of activity. Short-haired, long-legged men moved in and out of the opaque-glassed offices, military types who were obviously on duty. The sudden influx of personnel could only mean one thing—something big was going on.

The covert consulate was going hard.

At last, Bolan thought. They were closing in on Sinistra.

He stepped into the meeting room on the fourth floor. Hal Brognola was sitting at the black round table, hands anchored on a ceramic mug of coffee. The man looked like he'd been going nonstop for a week. He tossed Bolan a nod and waved him into the room.

Sitting across from Brognola like an overweight owl on a temporary perch was the man who'd been assigned to Bolan as occasional backup man and armorer. Roland wore a light tan suit that could easily fit a man and a half. And while Brognola looked bushed from working behind the scenes, Roland looked fresh, fat and well fed, as if he'd just returned from a leisurely vacation.

But they both had the look.

Something was coming down.

Bolan grabbed a cup of coffee from the pot in the corner, then took a chair to the right of Brognola. "What do we have?"

Roland held up a white envelope about the size of a greeting card. "Maybe nothing. Maybe everything."

"Invitation to a party?" Bolan asked, taking the envelope by the corner.

"Could be," Roland replied. "A courier delivered this to one of our dead-drops today. It tooks like the Giamantes have carried out their end of the bargain and pinpointed Sinistra for us."

"Looks like?"

Roland shrugged. "You never can tell with this kind of people. They're used to walking the tightrope. It could be bona fide or it could be a trap. Maybe they figure on luring you somewhere so they can take you out once and for all because you're such a pain in the ass."

"Maybe. But they came through for me a couple of times already. They know what's at stake." Turning to Brognola, he said, "What's your take on it, Hal?"

The big Fed nodded. "You're right. So far they've been right on the money. I think we can trust them on this. Otherwise, they know we'll come after them for real. No more tranquilizer shots."

Bolan nodded. Giamante knew he'd have to answer to him if there was a double cross. Besides, Giamante wanted the same thing as Bolan did. He wanted Amory Faust out of business and off his back. Preferably forever.

The Executioner reached inside the envelope and fished out a packet of glossy color photographs, carefully spreading them out in front of him like a deck of tarot cards to read his future.

The photgraphs were all taken at the same location, showing different angles of a cluster of buildings by a lake. There was a main house with a lot of sliding glass doors and a long wraparound deck. In the back was an oval-shaped swimming pool, sauna and Jacuzzi. Everything a hard-working terrorist needed for his off hours. Like stepping-stones heading down toward the lakeshore, there were a few more small buildings with a lot of white slat-backed chairs and lounges spread around them. A half-dozen late-model cars and a station wagon were parked in the long driveway in back of the main house.

Some of the photos were worm's-eye views taken from the water, apparently with a telephoto lens from a boat trolling past the shoreline. Other photos appeared to be drive-by shots from the road passing near the enclave.

After scanning the photos, Bolan picked up one that showed a wide shot of the main building.

"Take a look at the back," Roland suggested. "It paints an even prettier picture."

Bolan flipped it over, then read the neat handwriting on the back in the bottom right corner. *Lakefront property. A real steal. Must act fast. Won't be here for long. Come see Lake Maggiore before it's too late.*

"We're on the right track," the warrior said. "I hope." He flipped the photo back onto the table, sending the villa pinwheeling across the smooth surface. "Whereabouts on Lake Maggiore?"

"Close to the Swiss border," Brognola said. "Which makes a lot of sense if you're standing in Amory Faust's shoes. If something goes wrong, he can cut and run."

"Or swim."

"Yeah, Striker, we thought of that. That's why we're negotiating with Magnus to bring in a team from Comsubin. If this is the right place and Faust tries to water-ski his ass out of there, they'll cut his feet out from under him."

Commando Raggruppamente Subacqui ed Incursori, commonly called COMSUBIN, was the special forces branch of the Italian navy. Though the frogmen obviously specialized in naval operations much like their American SEAL team counterparts, they covered a lot more than the waterfront when it came to counterterrorist ops. In recent years they'd handled everything from airliner hijackings to hostage-rescue situations.

"I like the sound of that," Bolan said. "If we're going to have a war on our hands, it can't hurt to have the best."

"Right. That's why you're here, and why Roland is assigned to this operation. The two of you are in this until the end. Magnus wants it that way. He'll cut through any of the red tape to keep you on the mission. You're the ones who got us this far."

"Come on, Hal," Roland said. "You're giving me a swelled head."

"Need something to match that gut of yours."

"No guts, no glory."

Bolan looked at the heavyset operative. There was nothing about Roland to indicate that he was of commando caliber, nor anything to indicate how many missions the man had survived. But from everything Bolan had seen of him, Roland knew his stuff. He was good with weapons, both using them and delivering them, and he moved a lot faster than expected for a man of his bulk. He was also a quick thinker.

"Before we start congratulating ourselves," Bolan said, "we've got two questions to answer." He tapped the photos on the table. "Is this the right place? And if it is, have they moved the hostages there?"

"I've got people working on it full-time," Brognola told him "Twenty-four-hour surveillance on the target site. Satellite and overflight reconnaissance. Soon we'll have every last inch of that place miked and mapped."

"How about the Amicus connection?" Bolan asked. "Any leads there? That'll be the nail we need."

"We're working on it. Chances are whatever company is paying for this holiday camp will tie in with the Amicus company you told us about. It'll take awhile for our bean counters to push the right buttons and break the right arms, but they'll find out if we got the right place."

"It's the right place. I can smell it."

"You're going to do better than that, Striker," Brognola promised. "As of right now you and Roland are going on a vacation. Start packing your bags."

"Maggiore?" Bolan asked.

"Right. Magnus used his connections to arrange for some accommodations for you on the lake. Practically right on top of this little hideaway."

Bolan took another glance at the photos on the table. "Thanks, Hal. Looks like a nice place to visit."

"Yeah," Roland said. "But I wouldn't want to die there."

DURING THE NEXT FEW DAYS an influx of heavily armed "vacationers" descended upon Lake Maggiore. Some of them stayed at the small lake village resorts that followed both sides of the lake. Others moved into rooms of some of the grand lodges that had suddenly been made available to them.

Bolan was staying at a bayside lodge on the western side of the lake, about two miles south of the suspected Sinistra hideout near the Swiss border. It was an elaborate, rustic retreat just outside the resort town of Cannobio that belonged to one of Corbin Magnus's friends in the media. The man was friend enough to offer use of the premises with no questions asked.

On the ground floor of the retreat were several suites with floor-to-ceiling windows, each one with a private bath. On the second floor was a music room, a dining room fit for fifty, and an observatory with telescope the owner used to watch the heavens above—or the heavenly bodies on the lake.

It was outfitted like a luxury hotel.

But the guests—Bolan, Victoria, Roland and a few other men from the consulate in Milan—paid little attention to the luxuries. To them it was just another staging area for a cold war that was going to turn hot at any moment.

They turned a spare bedroom on the second floor into a temporary war room, covering the walls with a steadily increasing flow of high-resolution reconnaissance photos of the targeted villa and the surrounding area.

Bolan had pieced the photos together to create a large-scale map of the area. It looked like a huge jigsaw puzzle...with only two crucial pieces missing.

Sylvia Magnus and Giancarlo Condorri.

Every spare moment, the team inside the lodge went over the glossy photographed terrain, committing it to memory and outlining half a dozen assault plans and evasion routes their quarry would take.

There was always at least one team on the outside, taking advantage of the small fleet of sleek single-hull speedboats and sport cruisers that were harbored at the U-shaped dock and boat house. The crafts were outfitted with state-of-the-art surveillance and communications gear.

With Roland at the helm of the sport-fishing boat, Bolan cruised along the shoreline, fishing rod cast out onto the waters while he trolled for the terrorists. Rounding out the cozy picture of a group of vacationers was Victoria Celine, whose suntanned body graced the deck in a bright violet swimsuit.

Boats manned by other task forces sailed past the site on recon runs, getting the occupants of the villa used to a steady pattern of traffic on the lake. Water-skiers. Fishermen. Cruisers. All of them lurking just offshore of the suspected house, waiting until the word came down.

It came on the third day of surveillance, courtesy of Brognola's finance raiders.

The computer analysts and covert money-counters had been working nonstop on unraveling the threads that might connect the Lake Maggiore villa to Sinistra. Since the head Fed's men were masters at creating front companies and misleading paper trails, they knew what to look for, the twists and turns to take in the corporate shell game. It was only a matter of time before they turned over the right shell.

"We got 'em," Brognola said when his call reached Bolan in the lodge's war room.

"The villa's connected to Sinistra?"

"Yeah. Right on the money. Payments for a long-range lease and extensive reconstruction were drawn from a real-estate development company based in Liechtenstein—at least on paper. It's little more than a mailing address. But it has a subsidiary in Zurich that turned out to be the missing link. The mother company of both places was the AmicusCo."

"Who runs it?"

"Chief executive officer is a nonperson named Karl Struhoffer. Believed to be an alias of the man known as Amory Faust."

"We're on target then," Bolan said.

"Right. Which we expected all along. So what now? Knock on the door and tell them to hand over the hostages and we'll all go home?"

"The only knocking I'll do is with a sledgehammer," Bolan said. "But you're right. We're still not ready to move. We've got to step up the surveillance. Move in closer and mike every square inch of the place so we know where the hostages are when we hit the lodge."

Both men knew they had to wait a bit longer. It was tempting to rush in now and try to save the hostages, but that would get the hostages killed along with a lot of rescuers.

They had to watch and wait, plan out every step, every conceivable scenario that could transpire when they went into action.

It was like a domino effect. It had to be choreographed perfectly, one move leading to the next. Otherwise, the wrong domino might fall.

THREE VEHICLES LEFT the Sinistra compound on Lake Maggiore shortly past midnight. Four men traveled in the light brown Volvo station wagon that took the lead, the two men rode in each of the black sedans that were the backup.

Moving slowly and quietly in the dead of night, they appeared to attract no notice as they pulled away from the lakeside villa, its glass walls shining like a giant amber lantern on the hillside.

But from the moment they reached the end of the driveway and turned onto the road leading down to the resort town of Cannero Riviera, they were followed by a covert caravan of experienced drivers Brognola had dispatched from the consulate in Milan.

While the land-based surveillance team followed with dimmed lights, a pair of black-flight choppers hovered above the Sinistra exodus, well out of sight and sound range.

To cut down the chance of detection, the Nightfox choppers were equipped with four-bladed quiet tail rotors that reduced their sound signature.

The choppers were also outfitted with 7.62 mm chain guns on the fuselage and thermal-imaging systems on the nose. The pilots wore night goggles that helped them track their prey over the midnight landscape. There was no way the clansmen would get out of their sight.

ALESANDRO VERGA SAT in the front passenger seat of the Volvo as it rolled southward at a leisurely pace, its headlights staggering across the spindly arms of the shadowy groves that spread out on both sides of the lake.

The air that rushed through the open window was cool and rich with moisture from the water, thick with the scent of the lush greenery rushing by them.

Verga was dressed in a white shirt, with a black suit jacket tailored for his underarm holster. He looked ready for a board meeting or a night on the town and perhaps even a quiet service in one of the churches that surrounded the lake.

Looks were important to Verga, something a lot of the new guys didn't understand. A man who wished to succeed in the organization always had to look prepared to do business. Whether it was a conversation or a confrontation, he had to look like someone to be taken seriously. Someone ready to put everything on the line.

Which was exactly what he was doing tonight.

Verga paid little attention to the surroundings that flashed by him. He'd fallen into his customary silence as he contemplated this night's mission. By commanding this phase of the operation, he was being given a chance to climb back into the good graces of the Sinistra organization.

It was also a chance to hang himself, he thought.

But at least he had his own handpicked crew working for him, men who'd been with him ever since the days when he was Sinistra's pointman for this kind of operation.

The days before he screwed up and Amory Faust stepped into his shoes.

His driver, an aristocratic berserker named Nicky, idly spun the steering wheel around hairpin turns with one hand while his other hand endlessly fiddled with the radio's tuning knob, pulling in snatches of news, bursts of static and pop music that streamed from the front and rear stereo speakers.

Verga tuned out the noise. He didn't really mind it. Nicky was the best driver he had, and because of that all other sins were forgiven. Besides, it was just a matter of focus. When he had his mind set on something, nothing could disturb him.

But it could disturb the men who rode in the back seat, Vincent and Serge, a pair of muscle-bound bookends who did what they were told, no questions asked. They were portable slabs of stone who had backed Verga through his rise and fall in Sinistra.

Serge gripped the headrest behind Nicky and made one of his typically subtle requests. "Turn that goddamn noise off before I break your neck."

"You wouldn't dare."

"Think so?"

"That's right," Nicky replied. "Kill me and you'll have to walk home. Neither one of you gorillas can drive worth a damn. And Sandro's got better things to do than run a car pool for great apes. Isn't that right, Sandro?"

"Right," Verga said by reflex while Nicky changed the station yet another time.

Verga shook his head. This was just one of the usual routines the crew had fallen into over the years, typical macho posturing that helped them kill time. Listening to them was like listening to one of the songs on the radio. It hardly ever changed, but none of them seemed to tire of it.

Nicky fell into one of his trances, eyes on the road, hands on the radio dial while he searched for some rock and roll nirvana that was always just out of reach.

Serge and Vincent fell back in their seats and loudly debated the best way to kill loudmouth drivers.

And Verga thought about his impending victory. Or maybe it was his impending doom. He was ready for either.

If everything went right at this stage, the name of Alessandro Verga would gain some more respect. He would be tossed a bone or two, maybe a higher cut than expected, a slap on the back and a good word from on high.

And Amory Faust would get all the credit.

It wasn't fair. As usual.

Faust would bask in the glory while it was Verga who had to walk through the fire. Faust had taken the easy part for himself, whacking a couple of civilians and abducting a pair of gift-wrapped turkeys. When things started getting a bit tricky, Faust delegated the handoff details to Verga. He was the one risking capture or worse—these days the Carabinieri and the leatherheads weren't that keen on taking prisoners. They took heads instead, every chance they got.

The hell with it, he thought, dismissing the bitterness creeping up on him. He couldn't afford to dwell on it now. Besides, he should be used to it. This was the price he had to pay for his mistakes in the past. If he ever wanted to be his own man again, he would have to earn that right.

This night was just one more long drive on the way to the top.

They rode about ten miles to the south, slowing when they passed through the lakeside resort of Cannero Riviera.

Nicky finally pulled up in front of a street-front nightclub with music and brightly clad women spilling out the canopied entrance. He turned off the engine, dimmed the lights, then after waiting a minute, suddenly switched on the ignition and pulled away from the club while Serge and Vincent checked for anyone tailing them.

The driver repeated the maneuver several more times, playing hide-and-seek with unseen shadows until he was satisfied they weren't under surveillance. Then he picked up the pace once more and roared away from the town, driving west at a steady pace that rapidly put another twenty miles between them and Lake Maggiore.

Finally they stopped at a roadside gas station and grocery store that was closed for the night.

The drivers of the vehicles killed their lights as they rolled into the lot, then sat there silently watching the road until once again they were satisfied they hadn't been tailed.

Then Nicky eased the Volvo parallel to the walkway in front of the store, rolling to a stop across from two hooded phone stalls bracketed to the wall. The other cars flanked the gas pumps, each pointing in opposite directions.

Verga stepped out of the Volvo, carrying a small "phone phreak" unit with him about the size of a walkie-talkie. After hooking the black box to the phone receiver, he pressed a button on the keypad that produced a high-pitched tone. A few moments later, Verga began hitchhiking on the phone circuits, electronically masking the source of the call to make it look like it came from Milan.

"Come on, come on," he said, listening to the phone ring several times. "Pick up the phone...."

IN HIS STATELY PALAZZO a few miles southwest of Milan, Corbin Magnus was walking restlessly down the dimly lighted gallery that led from his library to his office, when the phone started to ring.

He was wide awake, but the sound of the phone still hit him like a hammer, each ring sending a hollow chill up and down his chest. Magnus hadn't been sleeping well lately. He hadn't been doing anything well lately, trapped in a house that now seemed haunted. Everywhere he looked he saw his daughter, Sylvia.

His memory painted her image walking beside him or sitting in a chair reading one of the magazines from the Magnus fold. He saw her standing in his office looking out the window at the bell tower of Chiaravalle Abbey.

But when the phone rang over and over, he saw her imprisoned somewhere in a dark loathsome prison fashioned out of his worst nightmares. He knew too well what kind of conditions and conditioning kidnap victims had to endure.

Magnus walked into his office a step behind the Carabinieri officer on duty, and headed for his desk. He waited for the officer's signal that the recording gear was ready, then picked up the phone.

"Yes?"

"Listen closely, Corbin Magnus," began the refined but commanding voice. "This is about your daughter."

"Who is this?"

"This is the only man on earth who can help you keep your daughter alive. Do you understand?"

Magnus looked at the Carabinieri officer who flashed a hand signal at him that they'd previously worked out.

"I understand. If you are who you say you are. But how do I know you're the right one? Many people can reach me at this number."

"All right," the man said, a coldness wrapping around his voice. "We sent you a number of taped instructions." He described the packaging of the tapes and how they were spliced together, then repeated the demands they'd made upon Magnus on how to gather and bundle the ransom money.

Both Magnus and Condorri had been instructed to assemble packets of money in specific denominations that amounted to nearly one million dollars apiece and apportion them in several satchels.

"Satisfied?"

"Yes."

"Good. Then listen carefully. The time has come to make the handoff. We will do it in a series of four exchanges. You will be called with instructions about how to pay the first half of your money tomorrow. Condorri will pay his half the next day. It is necessary to do it in stages like this in order to demonstrate your good faith."

Magnus's face turned red with anger at the insult. The idea of having to show good faith to a clan of killers and thieves sickened him. But he kept his voice even as he said, "I'll have the money ready."

"Good. You will be instructed where to make the first drop-off. And you must come alone."

"No."

"What did you say?"

"I won't be there. I have a man ready to handle all of this, a negotiator recommended by my insurance company."

"Of course," Verga said. "Then he will come alone and unarmed. That way we all come out ahead on this. You. Me. Your daughter. The only one who gets hurt is the insurance company—and we all know they have much more than they need."

Magnus sighed with relief. And as the caller talked on, he realized that he, too, was relieved.

It was working out the way Magnus had expected. Kidnappers were used to working with negotiators and often expected it from their victims. The selected negotiator was usually a professional who was familiar with security matters and knew how to follow orders. His job was to hand over the money and recover the hostage. He was considered a disinterested third party who wouldn't be tempted to play the hero.

The way it worked was for the family of the hostage to get the ransom money together and make the payoff through the negotiator. Then the insurance company reimbursed the family.

It was nice and simple.

In theory.

But more often than not the kidnappers changed the terms in the middle of the deal. Paying a ransom was no guarantee that the hostage would be returned when promised. If ever.

"This is how it will happen," the caller continued. "You pay half the ransom. Condorri pays half the ransom. If all goes well, we will make contact again for the final payments. At that time Giancarlo will be released. If you try anything, the deal will be cancelled and the girl will not be released. At least not completely. A penalty will be exacted.''

Magnus waited. Then he realized the caller wanted to drive home his point.

''What is the penalty?''

''Very simple. Very fair. Very bloody. If you only pay half the money in good faith, we will send only half of Sylvia back to you.''

Magnus nodded. It was a foolproof plan for the kidnappers. By dividing up the payoffs and keeping one of their hostages in reserve, they could keep a strike force at bay indefinitely. The fourth payment might never be asked for. The girl might be released before a demand was made for the final payoff. And the kidnappers would vanish. Perhaps, so would Sylvia.

There was no guarantee.

''Then we are agreed?'' Verga asked.

''No,'' Magnus said. ''Not yet. There's one more thing.''

''What?''

''I want to talk to Sylvia. I have to know she's still alive before I go ahead with this.''

The man on the other end of the line paused. ''Do not make demands on me.''

''A request. I just want to hear her. The negotiator said it is always part of the process.''

''Your negotiator is good. Very well. You will hear her. But you will not talk to her.''

"How will I know she's still alive?"

"We will make a tape of her."

"The tape could be made anytime."

"No. The tape will be made tonight. And to prove that she is still alive, we'll have her read the headlines of one of today's papers."

"But I want to talk to her—"

"The tape will be played for you tomorrow. When we tell you how to deliver the money."

"I'll accept that."

"See that you do. Otherwise, the girl dies."

The man spoke with a directness that implied that he had done this before. His polite, machinelike and almost soulless voice was that of a man who would do almost anything if he was crossed. It was part of his crooked code of chivalry.

The law of the wild. This kind of people made their own laws and sealed their bargains with blood.

"I'll be waiting for your call," Magnus said.

The line went dead.

12

Sylvia Magnus had grown used to living in shadows. The damp and cool darkness was comfortable to her now. In the dark she had no fear. She was alone there in a ten-foot-by-ten-foot soundproofed cocoon that was permeated with the smell of the earth.

She had explored every inch of it, beginning with the thick wooden door that led upstairs to the main house the Sinistra clan had moved into. The door was bolted and barred from the outside and didn't budge a fraction no matter how hard she tried. From there she'd moved on to the slanted metal doors that capped the only other exit from her subterranean cell.

In the beginning she'd tried to claw and pry her way out through the metal doors. But it was no use. They were secure, almost as if the house had been built just to keep her there.

Like a mole hibernating in an underground warren, Sylvia soon stopped thinking about the outside world. At least here in the underground cell she was safe.

Unhurt.

Untouched.

So far the Sinistra abductors hadn't really mishandled her. But their threats were growing more and more obscene. Time was running out, she realized. She would either be saved soon, or she would be sacrificed.

It was in the early hours of morning when she heard the locks unbolted upstairs. She knew it was late because the house was quiet. Usually it was full of voices and the loud rumble of footsteps walking overhead.

But now it was hushed.

Keys jangled in the lock, and the door burst inward. Two men stood on the threshold, their shadowy forms backlit.

Sylvia recoiled from the glare, shielding her eyes until they got used to the flood of light and could make out which of her jailers had come to play.

The first man in was Faust. His predatory eyes looked at her disheveled condition with satisfaction.

But the man with him, the one carrying a lantern, appeared to be all business. She could have been in a crisp white dress or nothing at all and it would have been the same with him.

This one was apparently Faust's second-in-command. She'd heard him called Sandro before. And if such a thing was possible, she felt a bit safer when he was around. Not that he wouldn't hurt her if he felt it was necessary. But he wouldn't play the same kind of cat-and-mouse games that Faust thrived on.

Verga closed the door behind them, then, a couple steps behind Faust, walked over to the wooden table in the center of the room. He set the lantern on the tabletop, casting a hellish light on their faces, making them seem like monks in a secret church.

Faust tossed a newspaper on the table, then placed a small cassette recorder near it.

"Get over here," Faust ordered. "It's time for your audition."

She numbly followed his instructions and sat on the single wooden chair, then looked at the newspaper he'd spread out in front of her.

It was the latest issue of *Il Giornale,* a newspaper from Milan that now seemed like a letter from an old friend as she scanned the front page. This was the first thing she'd seen from the outside world since they'd taken her.

But Faust wasn't the kind of man to bring gifts. She looked up at the hatchet-faced killer. "What do you want?"

"Don't be so suspicious. We've brought you something to read."

"Why?"

"Just read it," Faust said. "Out loud."

Verga repositioned the small cassette recorder so the built-in microphone faced her, then flicked it on.

As soon as she started talking a red light began to flash on the sound-activated recorder.

She read the leading story about a massive rally in Milan staged by political and industrial leaders from the Lombard League, a well-financed and influential group pushing for self-government for northern Italy. Economic independence and political reform were their key demands.

Even though her voice sounded numb as she read in a dull monotone, she found herself once again waking to the outside world. And the fact that they had brought her a newspaper and were recording her voice meant that there was a chance that soon she might go back to the world.

A world that hadn't forgot her.

Halfway through the article Verga switched off the recorder, then gently removed the newspaper from her hands. "That will do for now."

"No," Faust said. "I think we need something more. Something to convince them not to cross us."

"We have what we need," Verga protested, standing there stone-faced.

"I'm sure Magnus would appreciate a personal message from his daughter. Something along the order of, shall we say, 'Please hurry. Before it's too late.'" His hawklike visage bore down on Sylvia. "Can you do that?"

She nodded her head.

"Turn on the machine again," Faust said.

Verga shrugged, but complied.

"Please hurry—"

Faust's hand darted forward and grabbed Sylvia's hair. He wound it like a rope around his wrist, then twisted hard, ripping an inhuman scream of agony from her lips.

The motion knocked her off the chair and onto the floor with a loud graceless thump.

Still holding on to her hair, Faust picked up the small recorder and slid it to the edge of the table where the mike was facing the kneeling girl. He nodded for her to continue.

Tears streamed down her face as she inched forward and said in a tortured whisper, "Hurry...before it's too late."

Faust started to yank the coil of hair once again— until Verga's manicured hand closed like a steel band around his wrist, holding it in place.

"Enough."

Faust spun and faced him, his eyes full of fire and hate.

But Verga stared evenly back at him and spoke with a soft but threatening voice. "I said that is enough."

"Remember who is in command here."

Verga nodded. "Yes. And remember who is carrying out the final stage. I'm in charge of that, and I say this is enough."

Faust released his hold on the girl, then stormed out of the room. Halfway up the stairs he stopped and turned. "Bring the paper and recorder to Giancarlo's suite. It's time for his performance. I'll be waiting for you there. That is, if I have your permission.''

Then he spun around again and clattered up the stairs.

Verga remained behind a few moments longer to gather up the tools of his trade. He helped Sylvia into her chair, looked down at her as if to say there was nothing more he could do.

After all, there was a war on.

13

A sliver of moonlight shone on Lake Maggiore the following night when Sandro Verga's caravan left the Sinistra stronghold once again. The surface of the lake was smooth like glass beneath a hazy curtain of mist as they drove down the shoreline in the same direction they'd taken the night before.

When they reached the town of Cannero Riviera, Sandro's driver repeated his evasive maneuvers, driving randomly through the streets to check for surveillance before leading the other two Sinistra vehicles westward.

They traveled the same route for several miles before pulling into the secluded gas station. With the confident air of a broker about to close a deal, Verga stepped out of the Volvo armed with his black box and the cassette recorder.

It was time to play the greatest hits of Amory Faust, featuring the backup vocals of Sylvia Magnus and Giancarlo Condorri.

Everything went smoothly. After electronically camouflaging the origin of the phone call, Verga played the tape for Corbin Magnus, who was stricken silent by the sound of his daughter.

The man was numb. An effect Verga had encountered many times before. Corbin Magnus was in their pocket now, and soon that would be followed by his money.

"That is all," Verga said, after clicking off the tape. "Have your negotiator ready to move out first thing in the morning. Alone. Unarmed. We'll call you with the route he must take. There must be no deviations. If he strays in any manner, then—"

"What? Dammit! Then what?" Magnus shouted as Verga stretched out the silence.

"Then that will be the end of the matter," Verga replied calmly in the tones of an undertaker. "The end of your daughter. You'll never see her again in one piece. Do you understand?"

"Yes."

"Until tomorrow, then," Verga said, hanging up.

The phone rang as soon as he cradled it back into the hook, and he jumped back as if it were a gunshot, startled by the shrillness of the phone. It seemed alien out here and most definitely unfriendly.

Verga looked carefully around him. He saw nothing but felt eyes upon him. And in the dark regions of his subconscious he sensed the distant sound of black wings beating in the air. It was an ominous sensation. Like a vulture or a bird of prey circling around him. The cause of that instinctive fear hadn't made its way to the surface yet, but he knew that he wasn't going to walk away from this one easily.

His men felt it too. All of them came alert at the sound of the phone ringing again, like a shrill taunt.

Verga glanced at his men. They were alert, ready to run or ready to fight. It all depended upon his signal.

The phone couldn't be ignored. It meant that somehow, someone knew they would be there.

His right hand slipped inside his jacket in a fluid and unhurried motion. He nimbly unholstered his Beretta Brigadier, a 9 mm Parabellum single-action automatic with 10-round clip. At the same time he picked up the phone, looking at it as if it were a bomb about to go off.

A moment later it did.

But the bomb was a cold and hard voice.

"Move one inch and you're a dead man."

"Who are you?"

"The name's unimportant. I'm the man who spoke to some of your Sinistra friends. The ones who disappeared. I'm also the man with a gun pointed at your head."

Verga clutched the phone reflexively, then started to look around the deserted lot of the gas station. His gaze swept over the dark row of trees on the opposite side of the road and the large waste disposal container on the right side of the lot, which was large enough to provide cover for a few men.

"That's right," Bolan said. "Everywhere you look there's two or three men with sniper rifles aimed at your head. The same goes for your pals sitting inside the cars. Everyone's invited to this party, Sandro."

"And what is the occasion?" Verga asked, fighting to keep his voice calm.

"The end of Sinistra."

"That might not be as easy as you think."

"Easy? It's already done. Every square inch of this parking lot is a kill zone. You're all covered from head to toe."

Verga cocked his head. He scanned the perimeter of the lot once again, sought out assassins in the trees. He couldn't see anything, but he could sense it. "How do I know you're not bluffing? That you're not only one man...one crazy man." His voice grew bolder, almost as if he had convinced himself.

"This whole place is wired. Right now about thirty men are listening to every word I say on their headsets. This same conversation is being relayed to our teams in Milan and at Lake Maggiore. Believe me, Alessandro Verga, we are ready for you."

The rear doors of the Volvo opened slowly and two heavyset men started to slide out.

"Call them off!" Bolan ordered. "Now. Or we'll shoot."

Verga shouted at his men. Both of them stared at him, but climbed back in the vehicle.

They were all on hold now, waiting to follow Sandro Verga's lead.

He spoke into the phone again. "Suppose I believe you for now. What happens?"

"What happens is this—you listen to everything I say. I think you know the drill."

"And then?"

"And then you do everything I say."

Verga nodded slowly, lowering his head as if he were capitulating, resigned to capture.

But then he dropped the phone and pushed himself away from the wall. At the same time he lowered the Brigadier and fired at the glass storefront where he figured the caller was hiding.

He fired once. A trio of slugs was drilled back at him, ripping the Brigadier out of his hand and taking the tip of his little finger with it.

Then yellow bursts of flame winked from the woods, looking like an entire regiment was deployed there. Flash after flash crackled through the less dark woods. Laser-equipped sniper rifles lighted up their targets, then blew them away.

Four shots in succession blasted through the window on the driver's side of the Volvo, coring Nicky's temple, knocking him nearly headless onto the passenger's side.

Serge and Vincent barreled out of the Volvo on both sides, ready to fire but not knowing where to aim. Before they even got their weapons into play, a volley of automatic riflefire swept them off their feet.

Blood streamed from their sprawled corpses like water from a sieve.

Serge's short-barreled submachine gun skidded across the blood-slicked asphalt, looking like a toy next to his giant outstretched hand.

A thrumming rotorwash swept over the lot as the pair of Nightfox choppers descended. They were black patches of destruction masked against the night, dropping like wasps ready to sting. The 500 Paramilitary airframe of the McDonnell Douglas copter was fitted with enough night-vision equipment to turn the night into day for both the pilot and co-pilot.

The lead pilot bore down on one of the black sedans that was making a break for it, almost reaching the edge of the lot before the Nightfox opened up with the 7.62 mm chain gun.

A few moments later the bullet-riddled car exploded like a tin can, metal and muscle whisking through the air.

The other sedan fared no better as the sniping teams zeroed in on it like a magnet, hitting it from all directions. The vehicle zigzagged out of control to the end of the lot before tumbling upside down into a roadside ditch.

Sandro Verga was paralyzed with shock. All he could remember clearly was firing that one shot. Then everything else was a blizzard of metal. First his gun was knocked out of his hand. Then the phone banks on the walls were chopped to pieces. Lead singed the air around him, sending him left, sending him right, causing him to sprawl on the ground while the mercilessly aimed volleys chewed a halo out of the wall behind him.

Finally it was over.

Both copters landed in the middle of the road, their lights spilling daylight all around.

Then a heavy silence enveloped the lot.

Men in black fatigues walked out of the woods like an army of specters. They wore flak vests and helmets with night-vision goggles, and they carried an array of automatic weapons that they'd used with awesome precision.

Then Verga saw a man in black step out of the front door of the station. He carried a Beretta 93-R at the ready and had to be the man who'd been talking to him on the phone.

The Executioner walked to where Verga leaned against the wall, holding up his blood-soaked hand.

"Let's try it again, guy," the Executioner said.

A paramedic pushed through the crowd of covert operatives, then crouched beside Verga with his kit.

"Not yet. No sense in wasting it on a dead man."

"But he's not dead," the paramedic argued.

"I'm working on it," Bolan said. "Go."

The paramedic stepped away, then slid between Roland and a gray-haired Carabinieri officer accompanying him.

Verga shook his head in disbelief. "You can't do this. It isn't right."

"Worse that that, this isn't happening. Officially none of us are here. When we leave, you'll either be riding with us in a talkative mood, or you'll join your friends a lot quicker than you hope."

Verga's chest heaved. He slumped back against the wall, then stared hard at the man in black whose weathered face and dark glinting eyes showed no quarter. "You're the negotiator."

"Yeah."

The Sinistra hardman scoffed. "You don't look like a man who handles insurance contracts."

"I execute contracts," Bolan replied. "But I do things my way. Whatever has to be done."

Verga looked around at the parking lot, which had been turned into a battlefield, and stared at the corpses of his crew. They were gone. Every last man who'd spent the past few years with him was wiped out. All because of Amory Faust, the man who'd replaced him, the man who brought death to the only family that Verga had ever known.

Whatever was left of Sinistra meant nothing to him now.

"Whatever has to be done," Verga repeated, nodding his head. "Yeah, I'll go along with that. Whatever has to be done."

Bolan gestured for the paramedic, who stepped forward again and began wrapping Verga's wound.

"There's not a man here who wants to see you walk away from this alive," the warrior said.

Verga nodded. "Yeah, but if you wanted me dead, I'd be dead by now."

"We want something more. We want Amory Faust. We want Sylvia Magnus and Giancarlo Condorri. We want you to give them to us."

"In return?"

"In return you get lost."

Bolan hated to make the offer, but it was the only way they could get into the villa at Lake Maggiore without getting Sylvia and Giancarlo killed. Besides, it could work out in the long run. If Verga ever got back in the graces of the Sinistra organization— or what was left of it—then the authorities would have a contact there, an inside source who had dealt with them in the past and would have to deal with them again.

"How do I know I can trust you?" Verga asked. "What keeps you from killing me after I talk?"

"All we got now are words or bullets. You'll have to take my word."

"Consider it taken." He began to talk.

Verga told him about the layout of the Lake Maggiore villa, the security measures, the conditions of the hostages, where they were kept and how closely they were guarded.

And he told him what time he was expected back at the villa.

Bolan looked at his watch. "Then we'd better get going. We don't want to keep them waiting."

"But how—"

Then Verga saw the convoy of vehicles pulling into the parking lot. There were half a dozen of them lining up parallel to the road. At the lead of the convoy was a Volvo station wagon, the same color as the one that was now pocked with bullet holes and stained with the blood of his people.

Behind the Volvo were two black sedans, almost identical to the Sinistra backup cars. They were followed by several more dark-colored cars that no doubt had been on the road ever since Verga had left the villa.

He realized this had been orchestrated every step of the way. His men never had a chance. Neither did Verga—unless this man wanted to give it to him.

For all these years Verga had considered himself to be at war with the civilized world, a man who lived by the sword.

But only now did he realize what war could be like when fought by real warriors.

14

An hour before the main assault on the Sinistra stronghold at Lake Maggiore, teams of Carabinieri and Italian special forces units filtered into the nearby houses that bordered the villa, evacuating civilians from the area under heavy guard.

Bit by bit all avenues of escape were sealed off on land.

Then the innocent-looking fleet of "pleasure" craft came into play. The speedboats and sport cruisers that had been so visible in this part of the lake the past few days began to move toward the target zone, sticking close to shore.

On board were men in scuba gear with microphones built into their face masks so they could stay in communication with the rest of the force.

The COMSUBIN frogmen were armed with everything from short-barreled Franchi SPAS 12 shotguns to Heckler & Koch underwater pistols that could be fired in the water or on land. They carried other weapons of war in waterproof rubber satchels that they'd bring ashore with them during the raid.

The command post for the entire operation was a rustic lodge built on the edge of a spearpoint of land jutting into the lake. It blended in with the surrounding forest and had the best possible view of the Sinistra site.

Inside the command post Corbin Magnus waited with two high-level Italian security officials and Hal Brognola while they coordinated operations of the various strike forces, staying in communication with Bolan's convoy every step of the way as it neared the lake.

THE VOLVO WAGON EASED to a crawl as it turned off the access road, then inched around the sharply curving driveway of the villa. Two black sedans behind the vehicle followed suit.

A shape stepped out of the shadows and approached the passenger's side of the Volvo. It was a rake-thin Sinistra guard with a pockmarked face. As the guard drew close enough to recognize Verga, he realized something was wrong. Verga was the only Sinistra man in the car. The rest were strangers he'd never seen before.

Awareness of the setup flashed on the man's face. He tried to hide his shock as he stepped back, but couldn't totally cover the surprise. He was schooled in brute force, not in the subtler aspects of war.

His mouth gaped open, about to shout out a warning to the men in the villa. At the same time his hand darted for the big 9 mm automatic holstered at his side.

Bolan's Beretta 93-R fired one round from the back seat, closing the guard's mouth for good. The silenced slug trepanned his skull and dropped him to the ground where he lay in restful repose with a dark red third eye in the middle of his forehead.

The convoy moved on.

Now that the guard was gone, the rest of the vehicles in the convoy closed the gap as the Volvo led the way to the level parking lot dug out of the hill.

Without making any attempt at silence, the men stepped out of the cars in ones and twos, slamming the doors behind them.

Only Sandro Verga stayed behind, handcuffed and gagged in the back seat of the Volvo where he would stay until the operation was over.

THE ROADBLOCKS WENT into effect as soon as the convoy drove by.

Before the vehicles had arrived, the Carabinieri road squadron had been playing musical vehicles, silently cruising the area past the Sinistra stronghold without attracting attention, ready to swing their mobile blockade into their assigned slots.

Now the cars and vans nosed to both sides of the road, moving with a precision honed by hundreds of hours of training and actual deployment in the field against terrorist and organized crime enclaves.

As the vehicles took their positions, they created a zigzag path that could only be driven through at a slow speed and under the watchful guns of carefully placed operatives.

Two Carabinieri Fiat 6614CM APCs, each carrying eleven-man crews, rolled to a stop on the left and right flanks, choosing positions where they could roll downhill to the villa, if necessary. The low-profile armored personnel carriers could strafe the compound with broadsides from their turret-mounted 20 mm cannons and small-arms fire from the side firing ports. To add some fire and brimstone to the fight, the crew could call upon half a dozen fixed-range smoke-grenade dischargers.

In case the crew was needed on foot, the APCs had narrow doors on both sides and a large ramp in back.

For a more mobile strike and pursuit capability, the Carabinieri force kept a Fiat 55-13 Armored Bus in reserve. Covered with steel armor plating and 27 mm thick bulletproof glass, the bus offered high visibility and rapid deployment of its ten-man crew.

Though there had been some differences of opinion when the battle plans were worked out, both the Italian special forces and Brognola's people had agreed on one thing from the start—they were going in with massive manpower.

Like most Carabinieri operations, a small army of specialists had been filtering steadily into the area until they owned every foot of ground for a mile around.

They were playing for keeps.

BOLAN WAS THE FIRST ONE up the stairs that led to the elaborate wooden deck surrounding the main house. Roland walked behind him, a Beretta Model 12 submachine gun slung idly at his side. The broad-shouldered man from the consulate looked unconcerned, almost relaxed. He was going on automatic pilot now, letting instinct take over.

Matching their pace were a pair of Italian commandos from Nucleo Operativo Centrale di Sicurezza. The two NOCS specialists carried sledgehammers and shotguns, tools used to open reinforced doorways.

If those tools failed, Bolan and his backup man had half a dozen grenades that would do the trick. There was no time to try anything fancy. They were just going to blow the door off and walk right in.

By now the men inside the villa had heard the car doors slamming, heard the expected number of footsteps climbing the stairs. They didn't hear the other footsteps from the black-clad commandos who were spreading out around the deck, silently taking up positions they'd rehearsed in their heads over and over.

At this late hour, according to Sandro Verga, most of the clansmen would be asleep or pretty close to it. The others were expecting a routine return of the handoff team. In fact, one of them had glanced out through the curtains as soon as the headlights of the convoy came bouncing downhill.

After seeing the Volvo and the other duplicate sedans, the curtain fell back into place. The men inside were relying on their outside guard to warn them of any threat.

But the guard was dead.

The men on the deck had slipped on their antiriot respirators, knowing that a war cloud of smoke and gas was going to descend on the site when they went in. The shaped eyepieces of the contoured rubber masks molded to their faces gave them the appearance of high-tech exterminators descending upon a nest of vermin.

After a quick glance to see that everyone was in position, the NOCS cammando raised the SPAS-12 riotgun to his hip and triggered the weapon. In less

than one second, four-high-explosive rounds tore
through the doorway. Wooden splinters sprayed in
every direction as the fiery blast seared through the
entrance.

While the thunderous echo floated out over the
lake in a doom-laden sheet of sound, the man with
the sledgehammer swung with the rapid arc of a
railroad spiker and brought the heavy mallet head
down on the door hinges.

The splintered remains of the door flopped inward. Bolan leaped through the shattered gap and
triggered the Beretta 93-R, spraying 9 mm slugs from
left to right in a deadly scything motion that knocked
two men off their feet.

They were caught standing still, their weapons
holstered and their hands busy with wine and ciga-
rettes. They looked surprised, then dead as they
dropped to the floor with lead stitches across their
chests.

Roland stormed into the room from the opposite
angle a split second behind Bolan and unleashed a
stream of full-auto fire from his M-12 subgun. The
fusillade drilled into a Sinistra gunner who stood at
the end of a long hallway, gawking at the gas-masked
visions from hell.

Then the hardman went down, kicked onto the
floor like debris carried away by a lead stream.

Glass broke all around the upper floor as the assault team shot and smashed their way into the villa, hosing the rooms with sputtering bursts of autofire. The staccato sound multiplied over and over as clip after clip paved the way for the attacking force. The black-clad men quickly mowed down anything in their way, then advanced into the once regal hideaway.

WHILE BOLAN'S TEAM was decapitating the top half of the Sinistra force, the COMSUBIN raiders and NOCS commandos simultaneously went into action, hitting the basement cells where Sylvia Magnus and Giancarlo Condorri were kept.

Like creatures from the deep, the black-suited frogmen had made their way up the shore, leaving behind a few men at each of the smaller outbuildings on the villa's grounds.

When the shotgun sounded from above, the rearguard of frogmen opened up like fire fighters in reverse, thumping smoke and HEAT grenades into the outer buildings and scorching them with long incandescent jets from their flamethrowers.

It wasn't pretty or gentle, but it was final. The buildings were taken out of the equation in a matter of seconds.

Up by the main house the land-based Carabinieri raiders joined with the rest of the frogmen and set up fire-support teams for the assault units. With sharp-shooters scanning middle-level windows through night scopes, the breach teams were free to move against the basement-level cell doors.

The entry on the left cell went like clockwork. In a matter of seconds the breaching team hammered and cut through the slanting metal doors, prying them open and dropping down into the cell, shouting for the girl to get down on the floor.

Sylvia Magnus screamed at the sight of so many armed men, but a part of her realized they'd been sent for her. She complied instantly and dropped down.

While two of the COMSUBIN raiders formed a human wall in front of her, the rest of them spread out and took aim at the door to the interior stairway leading down to the cell.

A few seconds later the door opened up.

So did the COMSUBIN team.

They fired as one on the Sinistra gunman whose duty it was to grab the hostages in the event of an attack, their sustained bursts wiping out the hardman in seconds.

The assault on Condorri's cell didn't go as well.

Two Sinistra snipers smashed their weapons through windows on the middle floor and strafed the ground below, drilling the hammer wielders from head to toe with automatic bursts.

The support teams fired back, killing them instantly. But then chaos reigned as the surviving Sinistra gunners dived out of windows, leaped off the smoke-filled deck, or slipped through shattered glass doors, firing in every direction.

By the time the breach team got into the cell, Giancarlo Condorri was gone and two Sinistra shooters were in his place, dropping three raiders before they were taken out by a grenade.

Smoke and gas hissed around the house, punctuated by dragon tongues of flame.

BOLAN WADED through the littered hallway that led to a recently built wing on the middle floor. Smoke swirled at his feet. Cordite fumes and tear gas tinted the air all around him, but the irritants were filtered out through his respirator.

It was like walking through an alleyway in hell ... and then, as he rounded a corner, suddenly looming in front of him was one of hell's wild-eyed denizens.

The barrel-chested and heavy-stomached Clement Lacazino was holding a Heckler & Koch 9 mm automatic in front of him like a divining rod as he staggered down the corridor. His huge gray mustache was wet with tears, and grit from the exploding house clung to his body. His eyes were running, half-closed from pain, and he was staggering like a poleaxed bull, squeezing off rounds at random.

His 9 mm pistol was pointed straight at Bolan and his finger was on the trigger.

Bolan dropped to the floor and scrambled out of the way while a gunshot cracked through the wall behind his previous position.

Lacazino roared in anger and frustration, squeezing off shot after shot while trying to follow the Executioner's route. Finally the thick-necked gunman made it around the corner, straining to see his quarry.

But the corridor was empty.

Then the hallway was awash in dust particles and splintered shards of paneling as 3-round bursts from the Executioner's 93-R chopped through the wall.

A moment later the shredded chips of wood were joined by shredded bits of bone and muscle as two more bursts ripped through the wall and into Lacazino's massive body, punching the enemy gunner to the floor.

Bolan stepped back out into the corridor. He'd dived into the room around the corner and fired through the wall, walking the 9 mm bursts from the Beretta down the hall until they hit paydirt.

Beams cracked around him as the ceiling joints started to give way. The house could take no more.

Nor could any of the fighters inside it.

Like animals fleeing a burning forest, the black-clad raiders and the surviving Sinistra gunmen spilled out into the night.

And in the back of the house Bolan came face-to-face with Amory Faust.

Faust had dragged Giancarlo Condorri out into the open, using him as a shield as he ran for freedom—until he'd seen the human wall of paramilitary operatives who'd sealed off every escape route.

He made his way back to the glimmering swimming pool, waltzing around the edges with the weakened Condorri in tow.

The Executioner came to a stop on the opposite side of the pool. He had instinctively drawn a bead on the ax-faced Sinistra chief with his Beretta 93-R, just as Faust had put a 9 mm SIG pistol to the young man's head.

"It's over," Bolan shouted. "There's no way out."

"Oh, there's a way out. Right through him." He jabbed the barrel of the pistol harder against Condorri's temple.

"No," Bolan said. "It ends right here."

"You're playing with his life," Faust shouted, his feral eyes widening, his temper building as he watched his dreams and his lakeside haven go up in flames.

Giancarlo Condorri, who'd been practically lifeless all along, suddenly shifted his position, ducking under the Swiss automatic pistol.

Bolan went for it.

"No!" Faust shouted, caught between trying to kill the hostage or facing the man bearing down on him.

He swung the pistol at Bolan and fired.

But the warrior had the Beretta stretched out in front of him and a 3-round flash of 9 mm lead seared the darkness.

Faust's shot went high, but the Executioner's shots drilled into his target's head.

The Sinistra chieftain staggered at the edge of the pool, his lifeless grip on Condorri breaking free. Then he tumbled headfirst into the pool, a dark cloud of red staining the water around his head as he sank into the hell where he belonged.

It was over.

The Nightfox copters and two Medevacs swooped down onto the enclave, popping two-inch Mk 5 flares ahead of them that lighted up the ground with an artificial halo before settling down in a rush of rotors.

In the eye-straining brightness, Bolan saw Hal Brognola moving downhill. With him was Corbin Magnus and Victoria Celine. They were heading for Sylvia Magnus, who broke away from her rescuers and stumbled toward her father.

Giancarlo Condorri sat up on the far edge of the pool. He smiled at Bolan, then passed out, falling right into the hands of one of the paramedics who'd been sweeping onto the villa grounds.

Bolan felt good for the first time in a long time. Giancarlo was free. Sylvia was free. Somehow that compensated for all the other ones like them who hadn't made it.

Then one of the co-pilots ran toward Bolan, clutching his arm and ushering him toward the copter.

It was time to leave.

Officially he'd never been here. Brognola would take over now. He would concoct cover stories, outlining every step of the operation without mentioning names.

It had to be that way.

Always was. Always would be.

As he walked away, Bolan caught the eye of Victoria Celine, who had one arm around Sylvia Magnus. She waved at first, then slowly closed her hand, one finger at a time, as if she were grabbing on to the last moment they would ever set eyes on each other.

Bolan waved back then headed for the copter. The ransom run was over.

TAKE 'EM FREE

4 action-packed novels plus a mystery bonus

NO RISK
NO OBLIGATION
TO BUY

The hunters become the hunted as Omega Force clashes
with a former Iraqi military officer in the next episode of

by PATRICK F. ROGERS

In Book 3: TARGET ZONE, Omega Force blazes a trail deep
into the heart of Sudan. Trapped and surrounded by hos-
tile forces, they must break out at any cost to launch a
search-locate-annihilate mission.

With capabilities unmatched by any other paramilitary
organization in the world, Omega Force is a special ready-
reaction antiterrorist strike force composed of the best
commandos and equipment the military has to offer.